# Pup! et cetera

# Pup! et cetera

DEREK UPDEGRAFF

*stories*

STEPHEN F. AUSTIN STATE UNIVERSITY PRESS
NACOGDOCHES, TEXAS

Production Manager: Kimberly Verhines
Book Design: Quint Charvis
Cover Image: Tristan Brewster

IBSN: 978-1-62288-310-3

For more information:
Stephen F. Austin State University Press
P.O Box 13007 SFA Station
Nacogdoches, Texas 75962
sfapress@sfasu.edu
www.sfasu.edu/sfapress
936-468-1078

Distributed by Texas A&M University Press Consortium
www.tamupress.com

This collection is a work of fiction. Characters, places, and businesses are the products of the author's imagination or are used fictitiously.

*for Jim Updegraff,*
*my dear dad,*
*1944-2019*

# CONTENTS

I.

# RELEASE FROM THE CERAMIC DOGHOUSE

Carl arrived home just after 6:00 pm as usual, on a Friday ending another long week. He set his briefcase down by the front door of their ground-floor condo and walked over to the china cabinet in the dining room to see if he'd been put in the doghouse. He had. And so he cracked a beer from the fridge and grabbed a microwavable chicken potpie out of the freezer. His wife Linda would be in their bedroom all night with a migraine. And he would settle in on the couch again.

It was his own fault she used the ceramic dog and doghouse to let him know whether or not he could come into his own bedroom. He'd had the idea on one of her bad migraine days. She'd called him at his office to let him know she'd be leaving her own office early, another killer migraine. She just wanted to crawl in bed and block out the world. Knowing he was part of the world, he'd said to her, "Hey, why don't you put that little ceramic dog, the one in the china cabinet, in its little doghouse if you don't want me to bother you when I come home. If the dog's in the doghouse I'll know you want the bedroom to yourself and I'll watch TV quietly, then sleep on the couch." They'd both thought it was kind of a funny idea, and it was kind of cute in the beginning, Carl coming home just after his wife to see if the glossy white and black Dalmatian had been put in its little red doghouse, but Carl was over it now. Carl didn't like feeling like he'd done something wrong when he hadn't. He'd started to resent the dog and the doghouse and he swore that one of these nights he was going to smash the damn things.

These days his wife put the dog in the doghouse about three times a week. Usually on Mondays, Wednesdays, and Fridays. Linda's migraines had apparently developed a pattern. Carl knew that her migraines were real. The poor thing had been suffering with them for decades, practically her whole adult life, but Carl was starting to suspect that on some of these Mondays, Wednesdays, and Fridays Linda was faking them, putting the Dalmatian in the doghouse just so she could have alone time in bed in their room. And his obedience disgusted him. He was a good boy, for sure. A good doggy staying outside of his own room when she wanted the space for herself. Even now as Carl took the potpie out of its box and stabbed the film cover with a fork as the instructions told him to do, he thought about opening the bedroom door to see what she was up to in there. Then as the microwave spun his dinner around, he walked over to the doorknob and squeezed it—as he had done a dozen times before—but he didn't have enough moxie now or before to twist and open the damned thing. What if she wasn't faking her migraine? Linda is sweet so much of the time, but when she's not she's really not, and he didn't want her to pick a fight with him over nothing, some unwinnable spat he'd end up apologizing for. The microwave beeped. What the hell, he thought, and then let go of the doorknob. She's probably just reading in there. Let her read. He'll eat and drink on the couch, then fall asleep, and then they'll both have a good Saturday together. Do something fun like go to a used bookstore for her or some of those antique shops she likes to buy knickknacks from. Things like the ceramic dog and doghouse.

He hung his sport coat on a dining room chair, and then his tie and dress shirt on another, and then his pants too, so that he stood there in boxers, socks, and an undershirt before grabbing his meal and heading over to the couch.

Sitting on the couch, Carl got to thinking that this damn dog in the doghouse thing had been going on now for over three months. It started toward the end of August, just after what Carl thought had been a good summer together. They camped in a log cabin for a couple days. They walked around the little lake down the street and fed the ducks stale bread. The Olympics were going on, and they took a break from some of their movie nights to watch the swimming and gymnastics and even a bit of the running, which Carl thought was boring but Linda seemed to like only after the gymnastics and swimming were all done. It was a good summer. But sometime in August Carl had the genius idea of being all sweet on the phone: "Just put that little ceramic dog in its little doghouse if you don't want me to bother you." And now Linda seemed to be exploiting that, and Carl resented this setup, him on the couch for so many nights, and one of these mornings he was going to talk to her about it. "Let's get to an understanding here," he will tell her one morning. "I'm starting to miss you, and I'd like to get things back to how they were. I'd like to be in there with you while you're dealing with all these new migraines popping up." Something like that. Probably tomorrow morning.

Carl sipped his beer and forked the peas, carrots, and chicken in his potpie. It was a comfortable couch. He guessed he didn't mind it too much. On the mornings after he'd been told to sleep on the couch, he'd put the coffee on and then slowly open their bedroom door, safe in the morning, and Linda would usually be up already, sitting up in bed with a fresh look on her face, and she'd say something like, "Come in, love." And then he'd kiss her and shower and get dressed, opening his side of the closet, and he'd be thinking that it was worth sleeping on the couch now and again to have her in such a good mood.

Next door Carl heard the pitter patter of feet across the neighbors' living room floor. He was amazed at how late they seemed to let their kids stay up sometimes. It was around 8:00 pm now, not too late, but some nights he'd hear them over there at 10:00 pm or later, running around like hooligans, jumping on things, maybe doing some wrestling. He'd be a stricter parent if he and Linda decided to have kids. Linda said they have two boys over there. The family moved in on September 1st. Carl hadn't bumped into them yet, which was fine with him, but he did remember seeing a large truck and movers carrying in all kinds of big heavy boxes one day after they'd rented the place. And then a handyman's truck for a couple days. Carl and Linda owned their condo, alternating mortgage payments every month out of their purposefully-kept-separate checking accounts, and when the Whimslys who used to live next door told them that they were going to rent out their condo while they upgraded to a standalone house, Carl floated the idea to Linda that they should pull their money together and buy the other side, but Linda said she didn't want to risk her funds, and that was that. But they shared only one long wall with the other condo, and they had vaulted ceilings with no one above them, so that was nice. And the one shared wall mostly separated the living rooms, but a part of it separated the master bedrooms too, which could be a mood killer if there was a noisy couple on the other side, which embarrassingly the Whimslys sometimes were, but that usually wasn't the case with Carl and Linda in the bedroom department, except maybe after some occasion involving champagne, and so far at least noise hadn't been a problem with the new renters beside them. At least in their master bedroom. Right now their damn sons were grunting and bouncing around in the living room still. Carl turned up the volume on the TV. Then he got up to get a second beer, popped the cap, and went back to his program.

Eventually the noise settled down next door. It was getting late, and Carl was lying down on the couch now, tucked in under a blanket, just about ready to click off the TV and call it a night. But the bedroom door wisped open at the other end of their long condo, and Carl sat up as Linda came out in her bathrobe, sauntered over to the dining room, and took the Dalmatian out of its glossy red house. She set the dog on the dining room table. It clinked on the glass top.

"Is everything okay?" Carl asked.

"Fine, dear," she said. And then, "Come here."

Carl was excited to be out of the doghouse and thought maybe this was turning into a champagne-type night, and he hurried up to her. And she was all sweaty. And he asked again, "Is everything all right, dear?"

She grabbed a hand and pressed it to her cheek. His palm cupped the softness of her cheek and chin while sweat nestled between his fingers. She left his hand there, and then she stepped back and unfastened her robe. She was in a one-piece bathing suit, the purple one he hadn't seen for years, and she was wearing what looked like at least two sports bras over the top of the suit. The outer one was black, but a light grey one crept out around the sides. Her breasts were significantly smaller behind the layers of sports bras and bathing suit.

"What's going on?" he said.

"Follow me," she said. "No questions now. No talking now. Okay?" Carl nodded, and Linda said, "Good."

She led him into their bedroom. Carl had been picturing her under the covers reading while he watched TV, but the bed was still made, the same as when they made it earlier in the morning together, tucking in the corners so carefully, smoothing the comforter flat before they each showered and left in their business suits, side by side, until parting at their cars in their designated spaces. Carl opened his mouth to say something, but he waited. Linda walked to her side of the closet and slid open the door. Her clothes were neatly hanging, as always, and all seemed to be in order until she ducked beneath the pants and jackets and blouses and disappeared. Carl walked deeper into the room and then crouched down at her side of the closet. There was a door, only two feet high or so, opening into the closet of the neighbors' condo.

Carl whispered, "Linda, get out of there. Are you crazy?" She didn't respond, so he said it a little louder, but still there was silence, and all he could see was a portion of what looked like an entirely empty closet on the neighbors' side. He got down on his knees and crawled through the small open door, feeling vulnerable entering someone else's space, especially while wearing only his boxers, shirt, and socks. The closet was indeed empty, and Carl stood up from his knees and cautiously slid open the closet door to peek inside the neighbors' bedroom.

Linda wasn't there. The floor was covered in gymnastics mats, blue rectangular mats just like they'd put over the basketball court for wrestling and gymnastics seasons back when he was in high school. In the center of the room there was a set of uneven bars. He walked up to them, the mats squishing beneath his socks. The lower bar was a little shorter than he was, and he was five-ten with his shoes on, and the upper bar was at least a foot or two over his head. He touched the lower bar with a timid finger, the way he would some delicate thing. "Linda," he whispered. "Linda. Hello. I'm sorry. Is anybody in here?" But no one responded, so he stepped lightly to the bedroom door, away from the closet he'd just entered through, and he looked out of the master bedroom, down the long hall that was a mirror of their own condo, and at the end of the hallway, all the way by the front door entrance, Linda stood in her bathing suit and sports bras with her hands up in the air.

The entire condo was set up as a gymnastics arena, with a vault and springboard and long thick mat in the open hallway, a balance beam and surrounding thick mats in the dining room, and tighter thinner mats forming a perfect square that covered the whole living room. The place looked surreal, so clean and so spacious, and oddly wonderful for being filled with the wrong kinds of things. Carl forgot about his wife for a moment, forgot about the oddity of the place, this setup, or how this was even possible, and without the fear of stumbling across some neighbors he supposed never existed, he felt now, in this brief moment, like tumbling around on the blue mats everywhere and even giving the balance beam a go. But then he saw Linda again, and the confusion and questions and even some of the timidity came back—Am I in trouble or not? he wondered—and he waited for a cue from Linda, and she nodded to the only chair in the entire condo, a plastic folding chair near the center of the place, where the living room and dining room met toward the center of the long open hallway.

Carl walked to the chair and picked up the small dry erase board and marker that were on it. Then he sat down and looked over at his wife, and she lowered her arms and began to run full speed with her bare feet gripping the laminate flooring, and Carl worried for her as she ran so fast, and as she jumped so quickly onto the spring board and touched her hands to the vault and somehow, somehow, went flying off the thing, nearly scraping the high ceiling, and managed what looked like two somersault flips in the air, her legs so close to her chest. And somehow after all that hang time for just a second or two, she opened up her body and landed on her feet in the center of the mat, taking an extra hop with her knees slightly bent, and then springing up straight, her arms in the air, her chest out proud, her smile wider than it's been in a long while. And she faced him like that for a few seconds, as long as the whole vault took, and Carl was still in disbelief. He wanted to tell her to be careful, but he knew better. She was running this show. This was her program. And she said to him, "Old school scoring. Write down a one through ten. Halves are allowed."

And Carl said, "I can't."

"Do it," she said. "Please. No talking now. We'll talk about this later. You agreed. No talking now. Write down a score."

Carl wrote down a "10" and held up the dry erase board.

"No," she said. "Didn't you see I hopped?" And she wiped away the 10, and she said, "Be serious. This is serious. Write down a new score."

Carl thought about it. She'd done really well. He still couldn't believe it. But there was the hop, or maybe it was even two little hops, and he was going to write down a 9.5 or a 9, but then maybe she was a little uneven in the air too—it all happened so fast—so he wrote down an "8.5" and showed it to her.

"Thank you," she said. "That's fair. That's a good score." And then she let out a breath, put her shoulders back, and said, "Grab your chair and scoreboard and follow me into the bedroom, please. We're doing the Olympic order."

Carl followed her into the bedroom, and she nodded toward a side of the uneven bars. He set up his folding chair where she'd nodded, and when he sat down he crossed his legs and even leaned back a little. She slid the closet door back the other way, and from the floor, on the opposite side of where the little door had been installed, she grabbed a pair of gloves. The gloves were thick and had those hook like ends he recalled some of the gymnasts wearing on TV. But he remembered those things being taped or wrapped to their arms, and instead of actual gloves they smacked powder all over their hands and bars. But here there was no powder, just thick gloves with the fingertips cut off, and his wife put them on, walked up to the shorter bar, faced her husband, then faced the bar again, and grabbed on.

She pulled herself up and her stomach leaned against the bar. Then she spun around once, slowly, then a second time a little faster, all while mostly keeping her legs straight and leaning her body into the bar. Then she did the same rotations but picked up a little more speed, and once she had that speed she let go of the bar and soared the few feet in the air until grabbing the higher bar. She caught the upper bar with the speed, grace, and agility that Carl didn't think possible for her. Not the woman who dropped pickle jars, jam jars, wine glasses, all shattering on the kitchen tile. And now on the upper bar she did a few more spins, and now she wasn't hugging the bar to her body but instead she was fully extending herself, arms, legs, everything all stretched out, and her feet missed the ceiling by a foot or so, right at the space where the angle forms at the highest point, and she spun and spun and built up speed and then she released, and Carl gasped for fear that she would smack her head, but she launched out horizontally, and in her launch she flipped once with her legs extended instead of hugged to her chest like before, and she smacked down on the pad with her feet first but then fell forward onto her knees. Looking confident, she sprang up, stuck her chest out, put her arms in the air, and faced Carl, awaiting her score.

Carl knew he shouldn't talk. He knew he should write down a score because she wanted him to. And as he thought about her performance, really all she did was spin around for a while. There were no paused handstands or other tricks the professionals did, just spinning and one transfer leap, but she didn't fall off, and she did that awesome stretched-out flip for the dismount, but then she fell to her knees, and it was probably not quite as good as the vault if the two could be compared, so he wrote down a "7.5" and showed it to her, and she nodded and said, "Thank you," and didn't give away any look of excitement or disappointment, and then said, "Please grab your chair and scoreboard and follow me to the balance beam."

When they were watching the Olympics every night three months ago in August, Linda would lean in close to the TV whenever gymnastics was on, and once when she was doing that, Carl took notice of how her toes dug into their living room carpet and her calf muscle next to him clenched as she absorbed the leaping women, and now as Carl set up his folding chair near the balance beam in the adjacent condo's dining room, he remembered the tensing of her calf and her strong digging toes.

She hoisted herself onto the beam and hung all her toes off one side. She was directly in front of Carl, towering above him while he sat even though the beam was only a few feet off the ground. Carl wondered if the beam was regulation length. He guessed it was about ten feet long. Their dining room table on the other side of the wall was seven feet long and fit easily into the mirrored space with a couple feet left on either side of the long ends. She raised her arms up, did this little jazz hands thing with her fingers wiggling in the air, and then she did an actual cartwheel on that thing. Carl remembered an Olympic commentator saying the beam was only four inches wide. That's crazy, Carl thought, and he mouthed, "Wow," but no noise came out, and now Linda did a spin this way and that way, and she did another cartwheel, and Carl leaned in and gripped his seat, and then she leaped into the air and tried to do the splits, but she wasn't quite flexible enough to do a full splits, but damn if she wasn't close, and she stuck the landing on the beam from that leap that was almost the splits, and then she did one more spin on one foot and a few arm spin dance moves and a few squiggly body moves, and then at the far end of the beam by the wall that is the shared wall with their home, by that end at the shared wall, she stood straight again and took a deep breath, and then she half ran along the length of the beam like a short-legged gazelle, and she cartwheeled off the end of it and twisted in the air and just stuck the landing straight on, her feet planting into the pad without budging, and she smiled so big and puffed her chest out again and faced Carl. And Carl, really blown away by all that, he jumped out of his seat and yelled, "Yes! Yes!" and pumped his arm in the air, then yanked off the marker cap, stuck it in his teeth, and wrote a big "10" without any deliberation.

Linda nodded and chuckled and did a little zany head shake thing, like a sideways bobble-head type maneuver, and then she gathered herself and said, "Please take your chair and scoreboard over to the floor routine area for the final installment of the program."

The living room area was at most twenty-five feet by twenty-five feet. It also had the vaulted ceilings, so the space felt big, but Carl knew the square-matted area his wife created was much smaller than whatever the Olympic dimensions were. And the mats looked just to be mats, no springs or anything. Wasn't the floor supposed to be springy? Carl thought. He started to get worried for Linda. Would she even be able to do anything out there? The ridiculousness of her bathing suit and sports bras and this whole setup stirred Carl as he placed the folding chair near the edge of the floor-routine area. Was she renting this place, or did she manage to buy it without him knowing? How much money did she have in that savings account of hers anyway? And what does all this equipment cost? And was all this stuff rented, or did she maybe buy it all, too?

Linda clapped Carl's focus back on her, and he sat, and crossed his legs, and observed her uneasily.

At one of the room's corners, she took a small sip from a water bottle and then pushed down the play button of their old portable tape player. Then she stood in the corner with her heels together and toes angling down the two lines of that corner, and she raised her arms more v-like and less parallel than the other arm raises, and then the music started, something fast and Russian sounding, maybe the Russian section of *The Nutcracker,* and Carl was amazed at how loud that old tape player was, or maybe he just now realized how quiet all of these minutes had been except for his wife's occasional grunt or slap against the equipment. And with the music on, Linda ran five or six steps toward the center and did two cartwheels to the other corner. Then she turned and faced the center again, gathered herself up, chest out, breathed deeply and sprinted toward the center, planting her hands on the mat and springing into a backflip, an actual backflip with her legs flipping over and touching down after a full rotation. She barely got off the mat. But still, a backflip. And then the music cut into a slow piano melody, and Carl imagined Linda using a blank tape and that tape player to stitch together this music sample from their CD collection, and he thought this new piece was something by Chopin, and Linda did some slow arm swirls and body swirls to the mellow music, and Carl wondered if she was feeling embarrassed moving around like that, but she certainly didn't look embarrassed, and she kind of sashayed over to the wall at the edge of the matted square, the wall that separated this place from their home on the other side, and she crouched down looking at the wall and put her hands on the ground, and then flipped her body over her so she was doing a handstand with her legs slapped up against the wall to keep her upward. And upside down like that, doing a handstand with the aid of the wall, she pulled her legs down out of their straight form, and made a V, and the music was slow, and she pointed her toes, and then she brought her legs straight again and pushed her feet off the wall to land back down on the ground. She sidestepped over to a new corner while doing some hand movements and arm spins to the music, and then she took a deep breath and looked to the center of the mat, and the music cut again to a fast beat, something salsa like, and Linda ran to the center, did one cartwheel and then one backflip and landed upright on her feet near the opposite edge. The music stopped. Then Linda faced Carl, her chest heaving, her cheeks reddened by her blood moving newly around her.

Carl got out of his chair and walked over to her, placing the scoreboard and marker at her feet. He looked on her with squinting eyes, the way he'd do each time he opened a door to the bright outside, narrowing his view to take in what he could while his eyes adjusted to such new light.

# HUSKY

His doctor says, "This is getting serious." His doctor says, "You've got to get more exercise. Your heart needs it. It needs its exercise." He says, "Go for swims. Go for hikes. It doesn't help that you work from home. Get a standing desk. Take walks around the living room between stints at the computer."

So Charles drives to the city pool on the next day, clocking himself out in the late morning. He eases in and swims a bit, then tires and clings to the wall before moving on again. Young kids bob here and there, floaties on their biceps, too young, apparently, to be in school, but old enough to mouth "whale" while he struggles down his swim lane. He knows kids piss in pools. He knows he's never coming back. He's cold, cold even though that little one mouths "blubber" while pointing at him as if he's in a picture book.

Charles sleeps that off, stops by his mom's nursing home in the morning, surprises her with cranberry muffins and checkers. She says, "A muffin from my muffin." He beams, says, "Thanks, Mom." They eat and play. They stand for a stroll. She leaves her walker by the table and chairs. She leans on him as they saunter the grounds, circling the hedge path and admiring the spring blooms of the Weeping Cherries and Bradford Pears. She clings to his arm and takes little steps. Her hands are like talons. Her skin is like damp paper over bones. She smacks her lips. She says, "Aren't I the lucky gal to have this fellow at my side." He gets her back to her walker, kisses her forehead, tucks the checkers set under his arm. He says he'll be back in a few days for his regular weekend visit. Then he returns to work at home, answering e-mails, opening clients' documents, editing, formatting, sending them back. His doctor's voice echoes, "Getting serious. Heart needs it."

In the dark morning Charles wakes and starts work at his computer. He clocks himself out at 10 am. He's stiff when he stands. He walks a few laps around his living room, but he feels ridiculous. He's overweight—not ninety, not frail. He pulls out his phone and thinks about searching *standing desks*, but instead he searches *hiking near me*. Then *Sycamore Canyon* pops up, and one Yelp user has written, *A mild hike*, and another has written, *Scenic. Good for beginners.*

Charles drives the few miles to the nearest entrance and parks in a little public lot. He passes through the gate and begins to walk the outer loop, avoiding the narrower paths that go down into the canyon. The outer loop is flat. There is green everywhere because of recent rains, but now in the late morning it's getting hot. Charles is sweating. His legs are sore. Fifteen minutes in he's surprised to see a row of backyards only a stone's throw from the public path. The backyards share a long cinderblock fence, but it's not that high. They all have pools. They are empty. He goes off path and walks through the brush. He approaches a house with solar panels on its roof and towering hedges on each side of its backyard, shielding the yard from its neighbors. The fence separating the yard from the canyon is shorter than he is. He rests his elbows on its warm top, his chest leaning into the sun-warmed cinderblocks. He says to himself, You've got nothing to lose. He answers himself back, You're right, I don't. He presses his palms down on the top of the fence and attempts to hoist himself up, but he doesn't budge. There's no way he can climb it now, but there was a day when he could, and not that long ago either. "Forget this," he says aloud. Over the fence, the water gleams. The sun is hot. Maybe it's the heat. Maybe it's the canyon air. Whatever it is, he's determined, daring even.

He huffs back to his car, drives to the store, then returns to the fence with a collapsible stepladder, four feet tall. He puts it by the fence, climbs up. Peering into the yard, he debates whether he can do the five-foot drop down. He's upset with himself for forgetting about the drop. He climbs back down on the canyon side, hides the stepladder in a bush, returns to the store, buys a second stepladder. Now with two ladders, he climbs up one side of the fence, then down the other. The house seems empty. The pool is empty. A hand dips in. It's warm. He doesn't have a suit. He kicks off his shoes. He slides out of his jogging shorts and sweaty t-shirt, then tugs off his socks, lays everything flat on the pavement to dry. He stands in his boxers, dips a toe into the warmth, is about to step into the shallow side, then thinks, What the heck? and removes his boxers.

Undisturbed, he swims naked in the bright, warm day. He's not himself as he swims. He's all confidence in this private backyard. He finds himself thinking about stuff from another lifetime, about kissing Melinda Arroyo in fifth grade while playing spin the bottle at camp, about playing football in high school because he was big and coach said he had the perfect build for a lineman, about his mother calling him "husky" when she'd take him clothes shopping, whispering to the saleslady, "My little husky man." And he finds himself thinking about the cruel beauty of language, about gravitating toward words in high school, knowing immediately what Ms. Parsons meant in English class when she explained "oxymoron" and the other kids said that it sounded like an insult, and then her asking for examples of contradictions in a phrase, and him saying, "Little husky," and her saying, "Yes," but smiling something more, smiling something more motherly, smiling something like: I hope the world is kind to you sometimes.

He tires after four laps of the sidestroke. Then he stops and bobs in the deep end, and when his feet can touch the pool's bottom, he bounces over to the steps and sits waist deep to rest. He needs to pee. He glances around as if to locate the outside bathroom building, and then he remembers where he is, and he looks again at the still house, the sliding glass door way up there underneath the patio roof. It's probably nice inside. He knows there's no way he'd walk up to the house. All he wants is this pool anyway. He'll leave in a minute, climb back down his ladders, hide them in the bushes so he can do this again. But still, he needs to pee. What the heck? he thinks, then squeezes out a little. He stops himself after that little squeeze. Then he thinks, It's okay, body. It's okay. And then he pees and pees until it's all out, and then he feels gross and swims away from the spot and finds that he has energy again and swims some more laps before getting winded again.

Huffing and euphoric, Charles climbs out of the pool and rolls onto his back. The sun beats down on him. His eyes are closed. He imagines it's about 1 pm. He's planning on doing this two or three days a week, showing up in the late morning and leaving in the early afternoon. The backyard doesn't show traces of children. He imagines a young power couple living there, childless and in their thirties like him, off working each day at their high-paying, super-important jobs, coming home in the late afternoon, then going back out to the gym, then coming home again and enjoying each other's perfect bodies, then maybe swimming in the pool under the stars, sitting in the jacuzzi with champagne glasses in hands before waking up and working working working for their stuff and working working working on their bodies for themselves and for each other. Well that's fine, he thinks. He does not envy their things, and he's growing used to the idea of being alone. He just wants this pool when it's not being used. He just wants to trim back down to husky.

Charles is about to get up from lying on the concrete. He's about to get dressed and climb up and down his ladders, but the warm concrete on his back is like childhood, and he figures he should air dry for a minute before getting his sun-dried clothes back on. He rolls onto his stomach and pillows his head in the crook of an arm. The concrete is warm on his belly. The sun is drying his hair and the bottoms of his feet. The sun has now dried the backs of his calves and thighs. It has dried his shoulders and back, and his hair is mostly dry, but there is still dampness between his belly and the other parts of his body smushed to the still-warm concrete, and now he is being bitten in the ribs by something. Now something is clawing and biting his flesh. His eyes flash open but cannot see yet in the forced brightness. But something bites again, and in his mind he darts to his feet and is alert, but the body responds slowly and does its best to scramble up, having been jarred from this comfort. And a man's voice says, "Get up. Get up." And now Charles stands there, rubbing his eyes, suddenly aware of his nakedness, covering his genitals with his hands while the rest of him remains unguarded. He squints his eyes and focuses in on a thin man with a rake in one hand and a phone in the other.

"I'm sorry," Charles says. "I'm leaving."

"I'll call the police," says the man.

"Okay," says Charles, still adjusting to the light. And then he says, "But please don't. I'm sorry. I'm leaving now. I won't be back."

The man raises his rake, pointing it at Charles. His arm shakes from the weight, and then he has to let it drop and the metal teeth clang to the concrete.

"You don't need to do that," says Charles, stepping backward toward his clothes. He sees now that the man is older, in his seventies probably. "I'm not going to hurt you. You don't need that rake."

"I should call the police on you," says the man. "Have you arrested."

Charles steps into his boxers, sees blood dripping down his side where the rake clawed him. "I'm really sorry," he says. "I just wanted to swim today. I'm sorry. I won't do it again." He puts on his gym shorts and baggy shirt. "Thank you for not calling the police. Just give me a minute for my shoes. Please."

The man watches him. The phone and rake are calm at his sides.

Charles slides on each sock, laces each shoe. He walks toward the ladders on either side of the man's fence.

"Where are you going?" says the man.

"Home," says Charles. "You'll never see me again. I'm really sorry about all of this. This isn't like me. I'm not myself lately. But you'll never see me again. Sorry. I'm going home now."

"In there?"

"Pardon?"

"Do you live in there?"

"In the canyon?" Charles pauses to see if the man is serious. The man doesn't say anything else. "No," says Charles, "I don't live in the canyon."

"That's good," says the man. "Neighborhood watch says there are homeless living in tents out there."

"Oh, I see. I have a house. It just doesn't have a pool. I was walking in the canyon for some exercise, and then I saw your pool, and . . . Anyway, I suppose I should never have climbed over. I'm really sorry." Charles walks to the nearest ladder and starts to climb.

"You can leave through the side fence if you want."

"Thanks, but I wouldn't know how to get back to my car."

"What?"

Charles climbs back down the same ladder and walks closer to the man. "I parked my car by the trail entrance. I'm just going to walk back down the path so I don't get lost. But thanks for the offer."

The man takes a step toward Charles, examining him. "What changed?" says the man.

"Pardon?"

"You said you're not yourself lately. Why is a young man like you risking being put in jail for breaking into a pool?"

Charles considers saying that he'd never thought of jail as an option, that at worst he'd thought he might get a ticket, and he considers saying that he feared belittlement more than jail, being yelled at by some angry owner more than getting arrested, and he considers saying that he just wasn't thinking about anything at all, that for some reason he was being impulsive, reckless, that all it took was a hand slap from his doctor and some mean little kids at the city pool, that all it took was a check-up saying what he already knew, that he'd let himself get more overweight than the standard jolly husker his schoolmates and collegemates and occasional girlfriend tolerated and even loved sometimes, that he'd just gotten in a rut somehow, that it was slow-building, that nothing really prompted it but aging and years of routine, that reconnecting with friends is hard when they're busy with kids, that making new friends is hard when old ones move away for jobs and spouses, that he has no siblings but always wished he did.

He considers saying that it doesn't have to take much for someone to act differently one day, doesn't have to take much for someone to think, That's it, that's the one little thing that's going to make me more myself again. But Charles knows that people want more than a shoulder shrug, want more than an I-just-felt-like-acting-like-someone-bold-today.

So he lies, saying, "I lost my child. I lost my dear boy. Some time ago when my ex-wife got into a car accident after his soccer practice."

"Oh," says the man. "Oh my." He lets the rake fall. He slips the phone into his pocket. "Do you want to sit," he says. "You should probably sit." He motions to the patio furniture near the house. He waves Charles over in his direction.

Charles stumbles his way, unsure of what he's doing. He lets the man take his arm and guide him to a chair. The two stand by the furniture.

The man says, "Let's sit."

But Charles takes him in his arms, embracing him, embracing the slim yet muscular man, pressing his face into the man's shirt, weeping, weeping and embracing.

And the man lets him sob into him. The man stands there with him. He holds him. He says, "I can't imagine." He says, "It's okay, son. It's okay."

# IN OLDEN TIMES

Devon's sitting over there with a bag of ice between his hands because he's the poor bastard who grabbed the hot potato out of the microwave.

Lilly had zapped it for five minutes. And then the microwave dinged and Devon reached in and grabbed the thing, his right palm and fingers burning against the hot potato skin. He shrieked and yanked his hand out of the microwave, but for some reason he didn't let go of the potato right away. Then he tossed it up, but his left hand cut through the air to where the potato was falling, getting beneath it out of instinct maybe. So Devon grabbed the potato again, this time with his non-scalded hand until it too was scalded, and he shrieked a second time before letting the thing thud to the linoleum. He darted to the sink like a madman and ran cool water over his pulsing hands. Lilly said, "Oh my," and scooted to the freezer to fill a bag with ice.

When he'd suggested Trivial Pursuit ten minutes ago, Lilly groaned and said, "Not that again. You always win at that. Let's think. Let's think of another game." They were three drinks in then. And then it just hit her. "Wait, you guys," she said, "you guys, isn't hot potato a game? Wouldn't that have been a game once? Some game played for kicks in olden times?"

After Devon had scalded both hands and Lilly had given him the bag of ice, she helped him to his place on the couch and then went back into the kitchen to freshen her drink. She was about to step over the potato but instead she dangled a bare toe over it, and then she gently touched toe to potato. And she said, "It's warm now. Let's try this, you guys. Circle up. But not you, Devon dear, poor dear. Watch how it goes this time." And Lilly passed the potato to Marcus, who passed to Krystal, who passed to Peter, who passed back to Lilly, and Lilly was about to pass to Marcus again, but she held out the warm potato and said, "Wait, how do we do this? How do we play this?"

And now Devon's still sitting. And Lilly has her phone out searching for games, telling the others how to play Hunt the Thimble, and Krystal and Peter are leaning into each other like loves do, and Lilly and Marcus are standing close to each other like nervous loves-in-the-making, and Devon sees it now, sees clearly for the first time that he's got no chance with Lilly. And he's got nothing against Marcus, just feels foolish, is all. And Lilly says, "You start, dear Devon. We don't have a thimble, so find something else to hide for us. Hide that potato. And we'll come back in five minutes and look for it."

The others leave the room, and Devon gets up from the couch. He thinks about hiding the leaking bag of ice beneath a cushion, but he's not mad at her either, so he sets the bag on the coffee table. And then he puts on his jacket, grabs the potato, and leaves the house. Walking the sidewalk home, he cradles the potato in his hands, not hot or cold now, but pulsing from this movement all the same.

# DOROTHY

Dorothy's got a headache, and her heart hurts. Her whole body's aching actually because her heart pain has been leaking out nonstop, filling up her trunk and limbs, pressing up against her skin. But it can't push past her skin, all that heart pain, so it stays churning inside her while she stares at her computer in her shared cubicle. She almost didn't come into work today, but she knew staying at home would make it worse, wandering around in her bathrobe staring at all the pictures of her little man. But he's not a little man anymore. He's a man man, sort of, two weeks into his sophomore year, and now he wants to live with his dad on the weekends since he moved back to Los Angeles from Pittsburgh. All of a sudden he wants to try out weekends and then maybe even split custody half the time, maybe even move in completely until he goes off to college. Let's just see how a few weekends go, her son said three days ago. Let's just start with that and then we'll see. Don't freak out about this, Mom, her son said.

So now it's Friday morning and her ex is picking up her boy from school this afternoon, and Dorothy's at her desk, not doing a thing, not even sipping her coffee, and Linda, her cubicle-mate, has been mostly quiet. But now Linda's on the phone again with the dog people. The doggy daycare people. And Dorothy can't stand it. Dorothy's ready to pop her one. But she won't. She'll endure her nonsense conversation like always.

Linda's saying to a doggy daycare person, "I've noticed Herbert has been by himself a lot in the corner. Could you please tell Jake to show him a bit more attention?" She pauses, and then the person on the other line says something, and then Linda responds with, "Well, it seems to me that Jake has been spending a lot of time with that new Pomeranian. But I know Herbert loves Jake. I know Herbert would like a belly rub too. Or perhaps a second caregiver could be put in with The Mini Miracles so that all the clients can be shown equal attention?"

Herbert's Linda's fancy dog. Some kind of show breed. More like her kid, thinks Dorothy. More like some weird combination of son and husband, thinks Dorothy.

Dorothy's been in the same cubicle with Linda for a year now. Their backs face each other. Their desks and computers mirror each other. But Linda brought in a second monitor from home. And the boss okayed it. He okayed her having the doggy daycare webcam up on that second monitor while she does her work. If your work slows down or gets sloppy, he said, it's gone. But her work is as pristine as always. And all day long she's able to sideglance at her fur baby. Her words, thinks Dorothy. *Fur baby.* She calls those poor folks all the time, saying what she sees going on with her fur baby: Was that a loose stool I saw? Was that beagle-looking mutt picking on my fur baby? Can you watch out for that? He looks like a bully.

Linda hangs up the phone. She says, "I swear I'd find a new daycare if there was another near by."

The doggy daycare is a block down the road. Super convenient for Linda. She takes Herbert there five days a week. Drops him off at 7:45 in the a.m. Picks him up at 5:15 in the p.m. Who knows what that bill is? Don't most people just leave their dogs in the backyard, Dorothy's thinking. Don't they just kind of let them be and then hang out with them at night?

"But I've checked," Linda goes on. "The only other decent place is twenty miles away."

Dorothy says, "Uh huh," then pretends to be typing something important, clanking her keys with an even quickness. Dorothy didn't know dog daycares existed before twelve months ago. Dorothy has put in three requests to transfer cubicles but keeps getting back a discrete post-it note with a frowny face and *All boxes full for now. but will happen in good time.*

Dorothy's staring at random words she's typed.

Linda says, "See that one there."

Dorothy turns to see Linda's finger pointing to her second monitor. Then she's tapping the screen. Tapping at some white fluff ball. "That's the showboat getting all the attention. And look, there's Herbert in the corner. See how sad my fur baby is. Oh, Herbert. Oh, he looks so sad."

He's a smudge in the screen's corner. A tan cotton ball. Faceless, nondescript. "He looks happy to me," says Dorothy. "Is that a smile I see?"

"His back is to us," Linda's saying. "He's looking out of the fence to see if Mommy is coming to give him some love," Linda's saying.

Dorothy stands. "Want something from the vending machine?"

Linda's staring at the fuzz in the corner. She's whimpering.

"Can I get you a soda?"

Linda doesn't seem to hear Dorothy. Linda's petting the corner of her second monitor, whispering, "Mommy's going to check on you at lunchtime. Mommy's going to bring a special treat and lots of snuggles."

Dorothy's had it. Her temples are still pounding. Her skin is sore all over. She grabs her purse, turns off her computer, all while Linda's sniffling and stroking the fuzz image of her dog-child-husband thing.

Dorothy's down the hall, down the staircase, out the door, and now she's in her car driving the block to The Paradise Pup Resort. She pulls into the parking lot. From the front entrance, the dogs aren't visible. But she hears them yapping. There's a tall wooden fence, and behind that one there's a second chain-link fence. The east yard contains The Bonny Bigs. The west yard has The Mini Miracles. Dorothy's pieced this together from Linda's yapping, a frequent complaint being that there should be a third yard for mid-sized dogs since too many non-mini breads end up in The Mini Miracles with her little Herbert. But Linda has raved about the two-fence system, which keeps sidewalk passersby from seeing the dogs and makes it so they can't escape when a worker goes in and out. Linda often talks about the importance of top-notch security for the precious fur babies.

Dorothy's turned her car around. Her rear bumper is twenty feet from where she suspects Herbert is hanging out in the corner. She reverses hard and knocks down the outer fence and then the inner one. The dogs are going crazy, yipping and yapping, running away from fear or running toward her car because they think they're tough little dogs.

Dorothy's out of her car like that. She's in there kicking away the macho little guys while searching out Herbert. The one caregiver in there, Jake, is running toward her, but he's got some ground to cover. And there's little Herbert, stunned but appearing unharmed, frozen while other dogs are escaping over the knocked-down fences or running to the undisturbed corners. Dorothy snatches him up. He growls, but she's not letting go. She throws him into the backseat and speeds out of there before Jake can even graze her trunk. In her review mirror, he's frantically gathering loose dogs while other employees spill out of the building.

Herbert's yapping in the back seat. He's spinning around like a madman.

Dorothy doesn't know if he's pissed or just excited.

"Soak it in," says Dorothy. "Get it out of your system. We're driving. We're driving now."

Herbert barks and barks and barks. He stays in the backseat. He stays standing, looks like he's on edge, unnerved. Dorothy drives on, saying every now and then, "Pipe down, dog. There's a better life ahead. Pipe down, dog." Her voice becomes a whisper, her words like a prayer. Eventually the repetition soothes Herbert, and he crouches down in the back, his body sinking down with his head still up, still vigilant.

Dorothy's driving to nowhere in particular. She thinks about what it must have been like for Linda to see her dog get swiped. She must have been staring at that damn monitor. She must have been petting her fuzz ball on the screen when a car's rear blasted into view, knocking the second fence inward and all but crushing her baby. She probably jumped to her feet. She probably screamed out in horror when she saw some blurry figure scoop up and haul off her stupid baby. Everyone in the office probably rushed to see what was going on, rushed to the cubicle to see what the emergency was. And did Linda keep staring at the screen in shock? Did she keep staring when Jake and the other goofballs corralled the loose pups and tried to prop up the fences? Or was she gone by then? Was she down the hallway and zipping off in her car? Was she running up and down the street outside The Paradise Pup Resort, yelling, Herbert, Herbert, fuzzy baby Herbert! Dorothy hopes so. Dorothy's not a mean person. Dorothy just thinks Linda needs a little perspective. Needs to get a grip on reality a little bit. Certainly, Dorothy's thinking, Linda hasn't always been this crazy. Her ridiculousness must have grown from loneliness. Dorothy's feeling bad now, but not bad enough to turn around and give the dog back. She's thinking she'll help Linda meet some friends when she's done with this errand. Help her meet a man, maybe.

She's been driving away from home, she realizes. Why's she been doing that? Her son's not coming back today. He's off to his dad's right after school. Their house is her house today. And tonight. And all weekend. She thinks about taking Herbert home with her for the weekend, but she doesn't want to be in that house without her son. She keeps heading east toward Arizona. She gets out her cell and calls her boss, says she's feeling sick, says she clocked in but forgot to clock out after she went to the bathroom to vomit. She'll be back good as new on Monday, she tells him. And she doesn't think her boss knows anything about the dognapping. And she doesn't think the dog worker would have been able to memorize her license-plate number in all the commotion. And Linda's never seen her car before, so Linda shouldn't be suspecting her, Dorothy's thinking. And the cameras don't actually record anything, Dorothy knows, because Linda has said they're just live cams so that parents can check on their fur babies. So Dorothy's not worried about getting caught right now. Dorothy's ready to play dumb on Monday when she sees Linda. She's ready to be all, My goodness! What happened? Are you serious? Oh you poor thing, this is an outrage!

Herbert's tense but still in the backseat. Dorothy says to him, "You can relax now." Dorothy says, "So what do you and Linda do anyway? When she picks you up. What do you do? Go to the store, run errands, or is it straight home so she can tell you about her day? I bet she talks to you a lot. I bet you like her voice. Is she weird? I bet she has pictures of you in school-photo frames. Here's Herbert in kindergarten. Here's Herbert in fourth grade. Oh how he's grown! I bet she dresses you up. I've seen your Christmas photo, Herbert. I saw that reindeer sweater and those antlers you were in. I'm sorry, buddy. I'm sorry, Herb. But I bet she always has you in little outfits. Am I right? Little Herbert in his evening coat. Little Herbert in his Saturday morning polo shirt. I bet you eat dinner at the table with her. I bet she plans all her events around you. I bet when she dreams at night and she's spooning you under the covers, I bet when she's got her body wrapped around you, when your warmth is steaming at her neck and chest, I bet she dreams about you being a real man, dreams about you being a little guy, maybe even a dwarf, a real little person she can care for and devote her life to, someone she can give pleasure to and maybe even get pleasure from, but she probably doesn't care about that, just wants to please her little man always, please him and serve him and keep him from going elsewhere. She disgusts me sometimes, Herbert. I can't believe she thinks that of you. You're a dog, Herb. Does she acknowledge that? Does she acknowledge that after she's done fantasizing you as a person she can love and be with always? I'm going to do something nice for Linda after this. I'm going to take her under my wing. Well, probably not. But I'll take her out once. I'll meet her out in the real world once. I've got time now. I'll have extra time now since my real son wants to spend more time with his dad. He just moved back, the dick. See, I'm good about talking nice about him in front of my son. I've never bashed him. Maybe I should have. I could have made my son hate his dad. But my therapist advised me not to, and I listened. But my husband never listened to him, not in the few times I got him to come with me. My therapist told my ex to try recording his games instead of watching them live. He said to my husband, Just record the game. Avoid it while it's on. Do another activity. And when it's over, then you can see the score and decide if you want to watch it or not. You can enjoy the game calmly knowing your team will win. And if you don't want to watch your team lose, delete it, or let the result sink in for a day or two, and then watch it by yourself at night when Dorothy and the baby are sleeping. But of course my husband didn't follow that advice. Of course he wasn't all anger all the time, Herbert. Of course he had his moments. I did marry him. I did love him. But my boy is better off without him. That man is too much drive, too much temper. And I could tell my son stories that would make him hate his dad. But I didn't. And he never asked. Is that amazing or not? I'm not sure. Is that unusual for a boy never to ask, Mom, why aren't you and Dad together? I really don't know. But my sweet boy never asked. And I never gave him a reason to hate his dad. And he's only seen him a handful of times. Just a handful of times, Herbert. A handful of times. And now he's already thinking about moving in with him. I'm getting Wally Pipped. My son's replacing me. Have you heard that, Herbert? My husband used to say it. My ex used to say it. Someone's getting Wally Pipped. It's a baseball thing. Or a football thing. It's about some guy getting benched. I'm benched. But I've been doing good. I'm a good mom. Irreplaceable. But I'm afraid for Sunday. But you don't get to know that. You don't get to know any of this. But you're going to experience some things. We're going to find a better place for you. I don't think you're living the life that you should be."

Dorothy drives out of California and into Arizona. She's talking to Herbert, and Herbert seems to like her now. He seems to think things are good between them. He's got a casual look about him. He's not quite lying on the seat, but he's definitely more relaxed than before, sitting sphynx-style with his arms outstretched.

She exits the freeway and stops at a motel in some town called Maryvale. She lifts Herbert off the seat, and he lets her hold him. Then they go into the office together. There's an elderly woman behind the counter. She's decked out in turquoise and silver. A real earthy hippy type. Dorothy says to her, "Do you allow dogs?"

"We allow pets. One pet per room. With a bigger deposit."

"This is a pet."

"I figured," says the woman. "One night?"

"Yes," says Dorothy. "Wait, two," she says. "Actually I think one is fine."

"I'll put you down for one. Checkout is at ten. Let me know then if you need a second night. Your room's not going anywhere."

"Thank you," says Dorothy. "That sounds good," says Dorothy. She pays cash for the one night and the deposit since she doesn't want to use a credit card. She's not too worried about getting discovered as the dognapper. But, all the same, she's thinking, Better safe than sorry. Better to avoid a paper trail.

Inside her room, she sets Herbert down on the bed closest to the bathroom. "That's your bed," she says.

Herbert sniffs the comforter. It's forest green with little swirls. He struts in a circle, struts like a little tough guy, chest all puffed out. Dorothy thinks he's about to piss on the bed, but then his circle-strutting winds down and he curls up in the center. He huffs. He snorts and then he huffs again. And then he closes his eyes for a nap.

Dorothy showers. She washes her hair, soaps up, gets all rinsed off. There's something about standing in a tub that's not your own, something about mini bottles of shampoo and conditioner and body wash, something about an environment that's meant for vacationers or lovers, an environment meant for happiness and discovery, for a kind of release. She clicks the drain stopper down so the tub can fill with water. She's standing, and the water is running down her hair and onto her back. It's corralling her ankles. And then she sits down in the tub and lets the water fall on top of her head. Then she leans back and lets the water trickle onto her stomach and breasts. The water builds slowly. It's touching her hips, not yet covering her stomach. She's touching herself now, closing her eyes, thinking about the goodness in her ex-husband, thinking about the way he'd compliment her when he did, the way he'd call her Dodo, saying, My Dodo coos like a dove, my Dodo's the prettiest swan in the bevy, and no one else has ever called her Dodo, and she won't let anyone call her that again, but it was sweet with him, and she liked it with him, and she would call him Ox, the baddest ox in the yoke, and now she's reliving his big hands on her body, her squeezing herself around him when she wanted to, and then she imagines a better version of him. She's focusing on a kinder version of him, and they're still together, still married all these years, and he kisses her softly like in the early days, and he's asking her about the mug she made in ceramics, listening intently to her decisions regarding the shape and choice in colors, and he brings up the poem she wrote for him on their second anniversary, and he says that he keeps a copy of it taped to his monitor at work, and he says how the lines help him get through his day, and he's holding her in their bed, and he's moving slowly, and he's reciting the poem, pausing to savor certain words and explain why they mean so much to him, and then he resumes and is whispering, I love you I love you I love you, whenever he isn't reciting the poem, and then her body shakes, and then she's done, and she opens her eyes, and the motel bathroom light is bright, and the water is nearly at the tub's rim, and she dunks her head beneath the water, and water licks her face, and water crawls out of the tub and onto the floor, and she holds her breath as long as she can, and then she comes up for air, turns off the shower, and throws all the motel towels on the floor to soak up the spilled water.

Herbert huffs when Dorothy walks into the room with her office clothes back on. He's staring at her, still curled in the middle of his bed. He huffs again. It's a low drawn-out sound.

"You sound dramatic," she says. "Anyway," she says, "I haven't thought much about him in a long time. That's all."

Herbert's quiet.

She turns on the TV, plops down onto her bed. She finds the local news. There's a story about some teacher's generosity. Something about winning some contest or other and then choosing to take her elementary schoolers out to a fancy dinner. But then that's over, and they cut to this reporter in a scarlet blazer with matching pumps, and the heading *Chihuahua Dog Gangs Terrorize Children and Elderly* flashes onto the screen. The reporter's saying how the stray dog problem in Maryvale is growing worse. Too many people abandoning their dogs. It's linked to the housing crisis and job crisis, and people are packing up and heading back to Mexico and leaving their dogs behind. Dorothy's thinking this news report must mean something for her and Herbert. Certainly it's not arbitrary. Some things are arbitrary. This can't be one of them. The screen is showing these scruffy dogs walking up and down sidewalks. Lots of Chihuahuas, but there are other dogs too, some medium-looking and some big. But lots and lots of scruffy little Chihuahuas. And they're strutting around like they own the place. And sometimes they're alone, and sometimes they're in packs. And Herbert perks up when one of the dogs barks on the screen. And Dorothy says, "What do you think? Think they'll let you join their gang? Think there's some initiation? That could be a good life for you. Living in the wilderness or in some alley. Not on anyone's time but your own. Making your way off the land. Off the neighborhood. Getting together with some cute little vixen. I noticed you've got your balls intact, Herbert. I've noticed that. Probably Linda was saving you to match up with some pampered princess. Some other whatever breed you are. But I'm thinking you should spread those genes around out here, find a good alley girl, someone who will bear you lots of pups, little gangster babies, and give you the companionship you really need."

The news report switches from footage of loose dogs to an interview with someone from the animal shelter. Then there are the interviews with the locals. A young boy and his dad stand on the dead grass of their front lawn. The boy says, "Yesterday I was riding my bike and I was some blocks away from my home and there were like five dogs chasing me and barking at me and I had to pedal real fast and I was almost bit but I made it to my driveway and then turned on the hose." His dad adds, "Yeah a lot of them, many of them, are running after kids. They're getting into yards. They're barking. They're roaming in packs of five to fifteen. The last time I seen six or seven Chihuahuas together with two big dogs just cruising down the street. It's hard for the kids with little bikes to get away. I even seen them chase a car and get run over." Then the screen cuts to an elderly woman sitting on a bench in front of her house. She has tons of pots filled with succulents. She says, "I don't mind the strays as much as my neighbors. I have friends who are scared of them. I just sit here and mind my business. I like watching them when the sun is setting. I don't think they should be chasing kids. But I do like watching them when the sun is setting." Then there's an interview with an irate old-timer, but Dorothy turns off the TV and says, "Herbert, we've got to check this out. We're going out now."

She takes off Herbert's collar. It's baby blue. His dog tags clink. Two tags show that he's up on his rabies shot and that he's licensed. Then of course the main tag, the one shaped like a dog bone, has Herbert's name on it, etched in cursive, and there's Linda's name and address and phone number on the back. Dorothy shoves the collar in her purse. She picks up Herbert, and he's still calm with her, letting her cradle him in her arms as she maneuvers them out of the motel room. Now she's walking down the street, holding him like a football, but she'll let him loose soon. She'll know the right spot when she gets there. The sun is almost down, but the streetlights haven't kicked on yet.

The sidewalks are empty. The shops are closed for the day. Some are even boarded up with plywood, like the vacuum repair shop and the flower stand. She wants to say, Ghost town, but she's worried someone might hear and get offended, so she keeps it to herself even though there's no one around. She walks quickly. She's moving away from the small business district the motel was in and toward open space. There aren't even many houses out here, and she doesn't see any dogs. Where are the dogs from the news report?—she's thinking. Where's a loose dog gang for this buddy to join? She wonders if she should turn back and find some decent neighborhood to dump him in, maybe somewhere where a non-lunatic dog owner will take him in. But she keeps moving in the same direction, and the sidewalk becomes narrow and then ends and she's walking down the shoulder of some road. And then she veers off onto a footpath, and she's thinking, Isn't it unusual that this dog doesn't want to get down and run around? But he seems content locked into her side. And they're producing warmth together at the side of her belly and at her forearm smushing him to her. He's molded to her, a little fuzz hump, and she doesn't mind him nuzzling into her since it's getting cold.

She's debating what to do because there aren't any dogs around. I can keep walking, she thinks. I can walk for hours and hours, she thinks. I've got time. But she doesn't want to abandon this dog without a few other strays to keep him company. Dropping him here alone can't be the plan anymore, not since she's been imagining him running free in a little pack, hooking up with an untamed gal who can bring out the animal in him. "I just wanted you to have friends," she says to Herbert. "And maybe the right type of female. I don't know what I wanted. But, yeah, I wanted friends for you. But maybe you had that in your dog resort. I guess I kind of wanted you to die. It sounds so terrible when I say it out loud. But actually, no, I never wanted that. I just wanted to take you away. I just wanted to hide you out here. But now we should get going. I'll drive us back to California, and we'll talk about whether Linda should get to keep you. Maybe you should sleep in my son's room now. Maybe you're mine now. Yeah, you're mine now. You can dig holes in my backyard and get in trouble like a normal dog. You can stay in the backyard when I'm at work, and then I'll let you in when I get home. I'll take you for walks sometimes. I won't talk babyish to you. I won't dress you up in a little sailor suit. I'll give you a normal person's home. Linda will have to deal. You're mine now. Let's get you home."

There are more stars out here than in Los Angeles. There is a crisper night air. There is more light in the gray. And Dorothy turns around to head back to her car. She's been walking what—ten, twenty minutes down this path? No Chihuahuas, just shrubs. No dog gangs, just wilderness past a tiny town. Time to head back, she thinks. "Time to head back," she says. "I don't know what I was thinking." And her phone rings, and she answers it with her free hand, and her son says, "Mom, I want to come home." Her son says, "Mom, can you get me soon? I was wrong to come here." And Dorothy starts sprinting down the path, saying, "Yes, I'll be there as soon as I can. Yes, yes. Just give me a couple hours." And she shoves the phone in her purse, and she's striding and she's pumping her arms, and Herbert slips from her hold and thuds to the dirt, and he yaps and then he heads after her, trotting at first and then galloping like a little madman as he falls behind, but Dorothy is flying, flying down the dirt path and then the sidewalk, flying all the way to her car, the night air licking her sweaty skin, her wet clothes clinging to the body that's driving her forward and doesn't feel heat or cold or guilt or pain.

DEREK UPDEGRAFF

II.

DEREK UPDEGRAFF

# DUMMY

This all happened back when I divorced Tom and moved me and Jimmy out to California. I took another job as a paralegal and left Tom to burn in Phoenix. The cost of living was higher, but I managed to find us a two-bedroom I could afford, which was important, because Jimmy was four and he'd had his own room for a few years and I didn't want him to have to go back to sleeping in the same room as his momma.

Anyway, things were settling in fine, but then one night Jimmy comes into my room and he starts wailing on me, like really hitting me, his little fists tight like avocados still on the branch. I yelled at him, Jimmy! Jimmy! Stop hitting Mommy! But he kept swinging and swinging, so I shot up and squeezed him tight and secured those flailing limbs, and I realized that he was asleep, that he was sleepwalking. He'd never done that before. I mean sleepwalking. He'd never hit me like that before of course but he'd never once sleepwalked in his life, so I didn't know what to do. I just walked him back to his bed, kissed him goodnight, tucked him in, all that, and then I conked out in my own bed again, right away because these were long days back then. But an hour or so later, I wake when I hear my door creak open and little footsteps, and then I turn to look at Jimmy, and *bam!* He smacks me right in the face this time instead of the body. Well that was that. I shook him awake, yelled, Don't hit Mommy! And he cried out, sobbing and sobbing, so confused, my little man. And I held him and I could just tell, I just knew, that he didn't know he'd been beating on me. Neither of us slept the rest of the night. I tried to get him back down, but he was confused, upset. Disoriented and restless, full of so much anger.

After work and daycare the next day, we had a good night together, good dinner and reading and everything, but then at night the same thing happened. I'm peacefully sleeping, and then *bam!* Jimmy is at my bedside just punching me. I didn't want to wake him because he never went back to sleep the night before. So I walked him back to his bed and tucked him in. But then of course I couldn't sleep. I was waiting for him to sleepwalk back into my room and look for his momma to beat on. And shortly after I'd tucked him in, sure enough there he was, walking in with his eyes open and glassy, open but too fixed, like they weren't darting around like an awake person's eyes. I watched him walk toward me and I saw his fist cocked and balled up, and it just broke my heart because my sweet boy wanted to strike me so badly, and I didn't have to be a genius to know that he was mad that I took him from his father, but if he only knew the whole story, and when he got older he would, but for now he was just anger, just walking anger, anger with a purpose, walking straight for me, and when he swung his fist, I caught it in my palm and I kissed it, but he yanked it back and swung again, and this time I let him hit me. I curled up in a ball and let him beat on me until he tired out, and then when the swings grew weak and hurt less, I walked him back to his bed and kissed him goodnight and he slept soundly while I lay in bed and wept.

The next morning, I took Jimmy to daycare, and he was all smiles and love for his momma because he didn't know what he was doing at night, and he was well rested since I didn't wake him up the night before. We said our *I-love-yous,* and then from my car I called in to work and said I was too sick to come in. Which was true in a way, since this whole sleepwalking-hitting behavior made me sick in my guts. My boy swinging at me because of his father's wrongdoings.

I spent the day wondering what to do. Just driving around, until I wandered into this older part of town. I'd never been there before. It was quaint, like Main-Street old-timey quaint, and there were these little shops: a bakery, a toy store with wooden toys, even a costume store. This all took place in the spring, and I wondered how a costume shop could make money outside of October, but then again there I was, walking through the aisles and brushing my hands against the costumes on the hangers. And then I saw it and it just hit me. The idea, it just hit me. There was this dummy slouching against a wall. It was heavy looking, and sure enough when I touched it and then pulled up on it, I felt that this thing was heavy, durable. The dummy's skin was canvas, and it was stitched together really well, and the stuffing inside was firm, really well packed in.

I dragged the dummy to the counter and left it in a heap there on the floor, and I told the girl, Keep that there for me. I'm going to look around some more. And I managed to find a black goatee and green marble eyes, and, I couldn't believe it, I even found a pilot's uniform, and I put those on the counter and said, These and that dummy, and I swiped my card without even looking at the total. I brought the clothes and accessories to my car first and then I slung the dummy over a shoulder and humped that thing slowly to my car too. I thought about putting him in the passenger seat, but I heaved it into the trunk instead, curling the dummy's body into itself so it would fit.

I went home and got the dummy ready. I glued the goatee to its face, then the eyeballs, and then I dressed it and stored it in my closet. After I picked up my sweet Jimmy from daycare and we did dinner, bath, and book, I tucked him in and then got my room ready.

I sleep on the right. That's my side. I wasn't switching because of him. So I turned my bed completely around, with the footboard against the wall and the headboard sticking out in the center of the room. Then I put the dummy in the left side, which was now closest to the door, and I crawled into my side and tried to sleep, but I was giddy on that first night. I lay there staring at the ceiling, and I became real aware of dummy-Tom's presence beside me, his mass drawing me toward him. I leaned over and took in his outline in the gray light, not touching him but getting pretty close, admiring how docile he was now, rigid but well behaved. I grabbed his thigh like he used to grab mine, then squeezed as hard as I could. I dug my nails in but couldn't pierce his uniform. He kept staring at the ceiling. I slid my hand under his pilot pants and glided fingers down skin. I dug my nails in again and twisted one through canvas, lodging it into his stuffing. I wanted to make him cry, but of course he lay there like a dummy. I slid my nail out and felt bad for him, then kissed his wound and straightened out my body beside his, the pair of us lying in silence, waiting to see if this would work.

When my little man came in, he walked right up to the dummy and wailed on him, swinging those fists all around, beating down on the pilot-dummy's chest, smacking him in his face, little knuckles connecting with the glued-on goatee. He even smacked dummy-Tom's pilot hat off. I watched the whole time. My son's eyes were open, and dummy-Tom's eyes were open, and each set was as unreal as the other, each as foggy in the dim light, each peering straight ahead without any side movements. But not mine. My eyes were alive, quick, darting back and forth. And when my little boxer tired himself out, I walked him back to his bed and he slept soundly the rest of the night, and so did I.

It took about three months of using the dummy before Jimmy stopped sleepwalking into my room. I kept it in the closet for a long time after, just in case. But the problem fixed itself. And I like to think that at some point in those three months of dummy hitting, Jimmy made the switch, made the switch in his sleepwalking brain to thinking he was punching his asshole dad and not his caring momma. I like to think that in those months of him punching the scratchy goatee and smacking off the pilot cap, during all those glassy-eyed stare downs, the tender skin of his knuckles and palms let him know who he was punching, let him know the real fountain of his anger.

Once, during those dummy months, my boy visited his father for a week in the summer. Tom was flying a daily commuter back and forth between Los Angeles and Phoenix. We met at LAX, and he flew Jimmy back to Phoenix and then started his vacation. I imagined Jimmy in our old house, Jimmy in our pool, Jimmy in his bedroom. I worried about him coming back to me, about him not wanting to come back to what I'd carved out for us, our small apartment, just the two of us. But the week passed, and then I drove back to LAX to get my son, and Tom brought him to me outside of the security entrance, and he was in his uniform since he'd started back to work again that day, and Jimmy ran up to me and clung to me, and I looked at Tom, and he was about to say something, but he didn't, and he half-waved to me, sad attempt at apologizing, and I waved back, and he turned to go back to where the gates were, and as he moved his head I thought I saw some bruising beneath his eye. I thought I saw some purpling there when he shifted around and left without speaking to us, and I never asked him about it on the phone later, and I never asked Jimmy about it because he didn't know what he was doing in those sleepwalking days, but I squeezed his little hands and thought about how they'd have to grow, and I said to him, Let's get you home, sweet boy.

# THE INCIDENT AT OUR LADY

1

Phil had Sheila on the mind when he walked into one of the BOYS bathrooms at Our Lady of Peace Elementary in West Russelsburg. He'd started his shift as Second Security Officer at 6:00 am, about an hour before most teachers get there, and about an hour and a half before the earliest kids get dropped off for the Before School Fitness Club, which was really just thirty minutes of kids running in circles on the field while one of the coaches watched, thirty minutes of free daycare and an earlier arrival at the office for the parents who didn't care if they made their poor kids show up sweaty for the 8:00 am Daily General Assembly.

Phil had Sheila on the mind when, at about 9:00 am, the school was quiet except in the classrooms and he'd walked down the quiet hallway in the main classroom building and walked into one of the BOYS bathrooms. He'd been thinking about her all morning, as usual, and he'd been thinking about their seventh date—set to happen that night—and the fact that he was now going by Phil instead of Phillip, all because on their first date, three weeks ago, she said in a nervous fast-talking first-date kind of jitters voice, *Phillip? Phil? Is that you? Of course it is. You look just like your pictures. And I'm sure you go by Phil, don't you? Since you're so tall and strong. Should I call you Phil?*

So of course Phillip was Phil now after that, wanting to be thought of as tall and strong, which he pretty much was no matter what you called him, but *Phillip* seemed to connote something else entirely to her, something other than tall and strong, and he really liked her and wanted to be perceived in a positive light, so now he was Phil, and now Phil was standing in front of the mirror in one of the BOYS bathrooms, looking at himself in the mirror, saying, "Phil. Phil. Phil," as he did each night and each morning and so often through the day to help the name stick—to help his name stick, he reminded himself—a name that sounded so foreign but probably shouldn't, he guessed.

Phil liked his job as Second Security Officer at Our Lady. He liked the quietness of it, the way people looked up to him, the kids and even the parents and teachers. And he liked the simplicity of West Russelsburg, and he thought he deserved this calm town and job even though his two tours were pretty uneventful—uneventful, that is, when he stacked them beside the stories he'd heard some of the guys in his company tell, and also the ones he hears every Wednesday night when he hangs out with the old timers at the Veterans Center. But people at the school looked at him like he was a hero, and Sheila did, and when he'd see her tonight she would again, and Phil was grateful for all this good attention even though he didn't think he deserved it.

In the BOYS bathroom, Phil stepped away from the mirror and went into one of the stalls to use the facilities. He was allowed to use the bathrooms there on the main campus instead of having to walk all the way down the hill to use the bathroom in the Security Check-Point Building. But the rule was that he always had to go into a stall even if he just had to pee. That way no parents could complain that their little boy caught an eye-full more than he should have. But Phil had a nervous stomach because he had Sheila on the mind, Sheila on the mind more than usual, and he sensed something special about tonight even though he had no ring yet or plans to say anything yet, but still, he thought, there was something about the way Sheila lingered a little longer than usual after date six, lingered a little longer after the hug and kiss as if to suggest, *Hey, maybe we shouldn't be parting quite yet Mr. Tall and Strong Phil,* and the possibility of them being together sent Phillip into all kinds of joy and his stomach into all kinds of nervousness, and so he was there needing the facilities, and he locked the stall door behind himself, and he pulled out his gun from its holster, and he set it on top of the toilet's water tank since once, some months back when he was a new hire, the gun in the holster clanged to the ground when he let his belt fall to the floor so he could relieve himself, and he didn't like the clang of the holstered gun on the floor, didn't even like seeing it lying on the floor, even though holstered, since some kid could be staring at it by his feet from outside the stall door. And so he set his gun on the water tank as he always did, and he sat on the toilet, sat and took his time, and he thought about Sheila, and he kept thinking about Sheila, and when he was done, he stood and wiped and pulled up his pants and belt, and he tucked in his shirt and latched his belt, and he opened the stall door and washed his hands, and then he exited the bathroom to walk his scheduled rounds at the fences bordering the athletic field.

2

In Ms. Rivera's 1st grade class, students glued their grasshoppers' large back legs to their precut abdomens for the second craft of Insect Week. After positioning the insect legs just below where he'd glued the abdomen to the thorax, Liam patted and smoothed the points of connection and then raised his hand high and straight because he had to go to the bathroom. Ms. Rivera assigned Aiden to be his bathroom buddy.

In the hallway, Liam and Aiden talked about how their grasshoppers were coming along, saying to each other that they had done good work, that they each liked the other's grasshopper so far even though they had been working at different craft tables. They also agreed that Insect Week had been the best week so far. The walk from Ms. Rivera's classroom to the BOYS bathroom was practically the whole length of the hallway. Only Mrs. Delen's room was farther.

At last they'd made the journey to the door of the BOYS room. Liam pushed it open, the boys passed through, and then Aiden asked, "You need to go Number One or Number Two?"

"Number Two," said Liam.

"That's cool. I'll tell everyone you just went Number One."

"Thanks."

"Sure," said Aiden. "So I'll just be right here. We don't have to talk or anything until you're done."

"Okay," said Liam, and he opened the door to a stall and went in.

Aiden leaned on the counter with the sinks, practicing some math on his fingers while Liam used the facilities. Twice Aiden stepped away from the counter and took a few steps this way, then that way, marching like a soldier with straight arms and legs, and then stopped and leaned back against the counter to keep waiting.

Then the toilet flushed and Liam opened the door and said, "Uh, Aiden. Uh, Aiden, you need to come see this."

"Uh, no way, man," said Aiden. "Wash up. Let's go. I want to finish putting my antennas on before lunch."

Liam exited the stall and started washing hands, squirting three pumps from the soap dispenser, then rubbing rubbing rubbing his hands together until they had doubled in size with bubbles. Rinsing his hands down to size, he said, "No. You need to see this. We have to talk about something." And he looked over at the stall he was just in.

And Aiden answered, "Gross," exaggerating the *ss* until he too looked into the stall and saw something black on top of the toilet's water tank. "What is it?"

"A gun."

"No."

"It is."

"And you just sat there."

"I really had to go. I saw it. And I thought, I should tell Aiden. But I was about to go. So I thought, I'll just go. Then I'll tell Aiden after."

"Okay." Aiden walked closer to the stall and peered in.

"Sorry about the smell."

"It's cool."

"So what do we do?"

"We need to tell Ms. Rivera."

"That's true," agreed Liam. "We need to tell Ms. Rivera. Guns are dangerous."

"Guns are dangerous. That's right. So let's go tell her it's here."

"Ok," said Liam. And the boys neared the exit, and Liam shoved a forearm into the large door, but then Liam stopped pushing the door and let it close on them and said, "Wait. What about Wyatt?"

"Huh?" said Aiden.

"What about Wyatt? Wyatt would play with it."

"Wyatt *would* play with it."

"We can't leave it here," said Liam.

"No, we can't leave it here. That's true. Wyatt *would* play with it. We can't leave it here. Unless his bathroom buddy told him not to touch it."

"But someone else might while we're getting Ms. Rivera."

"Okay. Okay. So you stay, and I'll go tell her."

"I don't want to stay with it."

"But you were already in there with it."

"I know. But you were here. Right there. And I don't want to be alone with it again. I kind of wanted to touch it when I first saw it."

"I kind of wanted to touch it too."

"But I don't want to touch it now."

"Me neither," said Aiden. "Guns are dangerous."

The boys thought.

"So are you staying here while I tell her?" said Aiden.

"No. Remember? I don't want to be alone with it. Besides, bathroom buddies stick together."

"That's true. Bathroom buddies stick together."

"Always together," said Liam. "That's the point. To stick together."

The boys thought.

Then Liam said, "Someone might play with it if we leave it."

"Like Wyatt."

"Like Wyatt. And we need to stick together. Because that's the point. In case something happens. Like what's happening. So we need to bring it to Ms. Rivera."

"Okay," said Aiden. "That sounds right."

"It's what we need to do. So no one gets hurt."

"So we'll have to touch it."

"We'll have to touch it. But we'll be gentle."

"Okay," said Aiden. "Gentle sounds good."

"Should we hold it together?"

"Let's hold it together. Gentle. Like it's a grasshopper. Or like it's a rabbit."

"Or Fuzzkins."

"Yeah Fuzzkins. Gentle so he doesn't bite."

The boys entered the stall together and stood on either side of the toilet tank. The gun lay on its side with the barrel pointing at the wall.

"That's the handle," said Liam.

"I know. But yeah, you're right. That's the handle."

"And that's the dangerous part down there. Don't touch that end."

"Okay."

"Okay. One of us can hold the handle, and one can hold the middle part."

"Two hands?"

"I think so. I think it's going to be heavy. Metal is heavy."

"You choose," said Aiden. "You can choose."

"Do you want the handle?"

"I'll take the handle."

"Okay," Liam said. "That's fine. That's good. You pick it up by the handle. I'll pick it up by the middle."

The boys looked at each other and nodded. They breathed heavily in their thin torsos. They each picked up their part with two hands. The gun rose. The gun emphasized the smallness of their hands, the softness of their skin.

"It is heavy," Aiden said.

"And it's cold," said Liam. "That's good. We're doing good."

The boys backed up out of the stall.

"Easy does it."

"We should turn."

"Let's turn now."

The boys faced the exit.

"We need to push the door."

"I'll use my shoulder."

Aiden leaned into the door, and his shoulder nudged the door open a space; then his left leg and foot joined in the pushing and then his hip. And the door inched open with each hip, leg, and shoulder nudge, and at last the boys and the gun sidestepped out into the empty hallway.

They stared down the hallway. Liam said, "Don't look to the side. If someone looks out of a door, just keep looking ahead. If a class looks out the door window, just keep going."

"Okay. All the way down to Ms. Rivera."

"We'll walk all the way down. And she'll take this."

"Okay."

The duo began their shuffle down the hallway, whispering to each other, "Good, good, good," and "Easy, easy, easy," as they took small and concentrated steps, small and concentrated steps that got them past one door and then another while Ms. Rivera's door awaited them at the end of the hall. The duo paced their steps—Aiden on the left, his palms pressing awkwardly against the gun's handle—Liam on the right, his fingertips perched on the barrel, little claws gripping what they could, holding up as much weight as they could to assist the tiring hands beneath them.

From the back the duo looked to be sheltering something, shoulder-to-shoulder, hunched inward, a pair of altar boys guarding their candle's flame as they pressed forward, feeling eyes to their sides while looking only ahead, feeling the growing weight as they neared and neared their threshold.

Eventually they will reach their destination, and they will open the door somehow, and they will walk into their classroom, advancing to the story-time rug, then stopping there in the center of the circle as soon as Ms. Rivera sees what the class is shouting about, as soon as Ms. Rivera raises her hand for them to stop, as soon as she says to Liam and to Aiden as calmly and as clearly as she can, "Wait right there, good boys," and rises from her seat, trying not to stumble or panic, saying as she's nearing them, "Wait right there, dear boys, and let me take that from you."

# IT TAKES A VILLAGE

The whole time Dave's been at dinner he's been wondering if these lesbians will really be able to raise their son. He's a polite and accepting guy, and he like his wife's friends. Hell, he thinks, they're my friends now too. He likes his new friends, these gals, but he's wondering if they'll be able to raise this kid—their kid—who's a wild boy like most any boy.

Dave doesn't have any issues with the setup, with them being a couple or wanting to be parents, like he hopes to be one day. That's good. That's fine. But damn, he thinks, that kid's out of control over there, a real spaz, smashing Matchbox cars into the wall, into the furniture, and he's just a little concerned for these gals, and for the boy. Just wondering if they'll be up for it.

His wife shoots him a wink because she's been saying how great he's been doing at the office.

Dave smiles and says, "Thanks. Still learning the ropes." But he doesn't tell these gals how when he's sitting in his cubicle he feels like running batshit crazy all over the place more often than not. Wanting to knock down fake walls and tear off his shirt. And he doesn't say that he envies the damn gardener when he looks out of his window and sees him, three stories down, pushing the mower back and forth, line after line, until the square field is trimmed and he moves on to something else.

"He has twelve ties now," his wife says to her friends. "Twelve, honey," she says to Dave. "I counted them the other day."

"Is it that many?" he says.

His wife's long-haired friend—my friend now too, Dave thinks— Jill's her name—she says how great that is for him.

The medium-haired one—Gale—well she's drinking a beer with him, one from the six-pack he brought, and he likes that she's sharing in that.

He likes that he's buddied up on this side of the table with her while his wife and her wife sit on the other side drinking a red pinot.

Now the boy's over there smashing some robots into each other. Then the robots team up and start to heave all the Matchbox cars into an empty dog bed.

Then it occurs to Dave that he can help out these gals. He can help out these new friends with their wild boy, so he says, "I hear it takes a village. You know, to raise a child. It takes the whole village."

And Gale beside him says, "I don't think so, Dave. Time will tell. But I don't think it always does."

# GONE

Keith pedaled down Manor Drive with his lawnmower in tow, wondering if Julie had seen a penis yet. He suspected she hadn't, and she probably hadn't touched one either, but probably most girls touch a penis before they see one, though he wouldn't know. So maybe she'd touched one. Maybe once in the dark at that summer camp she just came back from. But hopefully not. Hopefully he'd be the one to have that honor. But that made him nervous, even though he'd be a freshman in two weeks, even though Chris reminded him often that he had his penis touched in seventh grade the first time.

So Keith pedaled toward the Thompsons' wondering if Julie would be at the court again this afternoon to watch him and the guys play basketball. He hoped to make varsity as a freshman. He was good, and he knew he'd start jv, but he didn't know if they'd tab him for varsity yet, and he'd have to wait for the semester to go on a bit before practices would start and he'd know for sure. And also, dammit, he wished he knew if Julie had touched a penis at summer camp, because if she had, there was no way he'd go after her, but then again, she really blossomed in those weeks away and he could forgive her for anything she might have done but probably didn't, and anyway if she saw that he was the only freshman on varsity she'd surely forget about any penis touching or other matters that preceded their courting and eventual marriage. And screw Chris for putting the whole idea in his mind when he leaned over and whispered, "I hear penis touching goes on at camps like that." And were they not chivalrous men in high school now? Well, Keith was. Keith's mind was burgeoning with . . . with the sophistication of the likes of a Lancelot or an Obama or an unnamed stalwart figure who wears a brown or gray shirt without any slogans and says wise things only when the riffraff around him have gone silent out of stupidity/lack of wisdom. Clearly Chris's mind was stuck in middle school since he had not yet undergone the transformation known as maturity. But damn, damn, damn Chris for putting the question in his mind. But really, honestly, there was no way Julie did any penis touching at camp when there were probably so many crafts to be done, like making a god's eye out of yarn and popsicle sticks to hang on her bedpost, or making lanyard friendship bracelets. She probably had a lot of those to make. A checklist of girlfriends so as not to leave anyone out. And didn't they do archery too? Wouldn't so many of her minutes have been spent mastering the bow— squinting at a target on a hay bale, pulling back the string and directing her arrow into the center circle, playing the part of a female cupid while he was the helpless hay clump, his heart on display right there for the world to see, pierced with longing?

But if she had touched a penis? How could she do that? thought Keith. How could she do that to him when the stars above her summer camp must have spelled out his name while she lay in her sleeping bag gazing at the cosmos, not literally spelling them out of course, but rather suggesting them through a misty glow that somehow, somehow in some unspellable other language, foreshadowed their reuniting at summer's end in a new light that was something like love-at-first-sight but not exactly that since, in fact, they had seen each other many times before throughout the years of middle school and half of elementary school, since she and her family galloped into town in the middle of either second or third grade. But that was all different. And how could she have maybe done this to him when he'd been unknowingly waiting for her so patiently all these years?—all these years of not having his penis touched even though he'd not otherwise had the opportunity but really, he knew now, was being faithful to their future selves, a faithfulness that must have driven him not to pursue the physical contact that he thought he wasn't ready for only to discover now upon sight of the newly rounding Julie that it had been her future self all along fueling such virtuousness on his part to take things only so far when he was a boy and not yet a freshman as he now almost was.

He pedaled up the Thompsons' driveway furious at Julie, but also in love and now actually pretty confident that she hadn't even done more than make out that one time last year with that douche Steve. Fuckin Steve. But didn't he hear that was because of spin-the-bottle or some closet game and not actual affections? And wasn't he—Keith the soon-to-be freshman varsity basketball player—obsessed with Ginny at that stage of eighth grade and busy trying to learn the art of the seemingly-easy-yet-actually-quite-complicated French kiss? Regardless, Steve and Ginny were yesterday's news, and Keith and Julie seemed destined to be together as they entered high school having really developed nicely in their own masculine and feminine respective ways.

Keith leaned his bike against the side of the house. He wheeled his lawnmower down his trailer's ramp and started in on the front lawn. He did good work. He prided himself on straight lines, and he had a lot of clients around town. Soon the fall weather would kick in and his business would slow down. He'd done three houses already that morning and had one more after the Thompsons'. Keith wasn't saving for anything in particular. Maybe a car in a couple years. Maybe a diamond heart pendant for Julie in a few months if he ended up taking her to the Winter Formal if he thought that surely she hadn't done anything besides kiss one or possibly two guys before he entered the picture and swept her off her feet. He supposed that in addition to the heart necklace and the limousine rental and the fancy dinner and the Winter Formal Picture Package A, which would have an 8x10 for each of them and some 5x7s for their families and select friends and plenty of wallet sizes to go around—he supposed that in addition to all that, it would be wise to keep some of his business earnings in his newly set-up savings account to start growing a down payment on a little starter home.

He pushed the mower forward and kept straight lines. One line. Turn. One more line. Turn. Methodical. Relaxing. His hands squeezed the bail control down into the handlebar. The engine whirred. The blade whispered. He pushed with just enough force, propelling the machine but not too quickly, getting a mild workout in his legs and arms and in his core, not like that kid over on Thistleberry who uses a self-propelled mower and has half as many clients as Keith.

And why didn't he sense how amazing Julie was when they were lab partners at the beginning of seventh grade? Hadn't her hair smelled like some kind of flower from some kind of exotic place? Didn't she laugh a little like a hamster when she twisted the knob on their Bunsen burner all the way to the right so that a flame shot up a few feet in front of their faces? Didn't he find that adorable and want to nibble her ear and give her a foot massage after volleyball practice? Certainly the allure was growing then, but she hadn't captivated him the way she did last week when she came back from her summer camp for the wealthy. Maybe it was the horseriding? Maybe it was the pine air or the lick of cool mountain spring water? Regardless, when she sauntered over with Kelly and Nina and sat at the picnic table closest to the court, and when she smiled at him when he made a layup and then stole the ball from Dave and made a second layup, well, that was when Keith could tell that Julie was going to be special somehow as a freshman and that they were probably going to be the ideal couple that people envied when they'd hold hands in the hallways and exchange quick kisses at their lockers. They'd stay together for four years of high school and attend the same Division 1 college where he would get a full ride for basketball and she'd maybe also get a full ride for volleyball or maybe a scholarship for biology or geography since she seemed really into that presentation on Mauritania last year.

Finished with the front lawn, Keith started on the outside edge of the backyard. He went line, turn, line, turn, line, turn, making his way to the center. Then music sounded out over his mower. He couldn't decipher it exactly. He pushed the mower toward the large back window and some kind of fast salsa music grew louder. When he got close to the window, the glare disappeared and he saw Mrs. Thompson dancing naked in their tv room. Her back was to him. She swayed and shook and jiggled to the music. He stopped pushing the mower but kept it running, still squeezing the handle and bail control together, ready to look away and then pivot and push if she turned around. But for now she danced while facing the other way, and he watched. He grew hard under his shorts. It just happened. She shook her arms to the side like a dancing fool. She jumped and squatted and raised her arms above her head. Her body was round and firm and seemed to Keith like the perfect body of someone in her thirties or maybe forties. He knew he should look away, but he couldn't. He knew he should turn his mower, finish up quickly while staring at the grass the whole time, and slip out of there, pedaling to his next stop. But he couldn't. Not yet. He watched as she moved in time with the beat. He studied the curves of flesh, of muscle, studied the line of her spine. He couldn't get over how soft and firm she seemed, both at once. That was the only way he could think of it. Soft and firm. He couldn't get over that someone got to be married to this and rest his cheek in the small of her back while she lay on the bed reading or talking about whatever she did in the day besides dancing naked. And why was she dancing naked in the tv room at something like noon? And would Julie dance naked in their home after they'd gotten married and he was off at work? Was this something women did in the day? Probably very few, Keith reasoned. Probably very few women danced naked and alone in their tv rooms around noon.

Mrs. Thompson did another leap and landed with bent legs, and then she swiveled on a foot and raised the other in the air as she finished spinning and then faced Keith. Keith saw the triangle of her dark pubic hair and he saw that she had one large breast and one missing breast, and he jerked the running lawnmower back and the blade cut his left foot in half, slicing through shoe and skin and bone while he crumpled to the grass, screaming and letting go of the handle.

The engine cut out. The lawnmower stopped vibrating and the blade slowed to a still. Mrs. Thompson ran into the backyard in a turquoise bathrobe that made Keith think of seashell necklaces that were probably sold in souvenir shops near oceans. She scooped the crumpled boy into her arms and brought him to her. She had a cell phone to her ear and was yelling for an ambulance. Keith wondered, Did she keep her cellphone in her turquoise bathrobe while dancing? And did she always keep her turquoise bathrobe near her while dancing naked in case she needed to cover up real quick like today? And after she'd shouted the address and "missing foot" and "come come come," she tossed the phone into a patch of grass Keith hadn't yet mowed, and she whispered to Keith, "You're okay, sweet boy. You're okay, sweet boy."

But Keith's foot wasn't really missing. He couldn't help but stare at it while Mrs. Thompson squeezed his head hard into her stomach and rocked him and now whispered, "Shhhhh, sweet baby. Shhhhh, sweet baby." Half of his shoe still covered his foot's heel. Half of his shoe had been shredded to confetti and dotted the mower's inside wall. His newly shortened foot pointed to heaven, a foot split in half mid-arch. Skin and flesh and bone sliced in a line as straight as a sheet of paper because Keith was good about sharpening the mower's blade like Dad had taught him. And the other half of the foot? Keith knew it was blended in with the grass goo that stuck to the mower's inside wall. He'd scoop out the damp grass clumps from the inside wall after each mow. He didn't want to have to scoop them out now.

Keith had a hard time hearing above his wailing now. Oh, he'd been wailing? Was that why Mrs. Thompson kept whispering, "Shhhhh, sweet baby," Keith wondered?—her lips grazing his ear, her warm breath tickling his ear canal, distracting him somewhat from the fiery sting where his halved foot was ringing and ringing and yelling at him, This is what you get. Oh, shit, the air is biting us where we should have a skin barrier and toe troops and even a shoe shield. Or was "sweet baby" simply a term of affection? Well that wouldn't do, all this crying. He jammed his lids closed and focused on his message to himself—*Stop crying!*—but he was not in control, and his tears soaked Mrs. Thompson's skin, and Keith wished his tears were super glue, that he could be fused to this angel rocking him, that she could scoop him up in one arm and carry him with ease, walking around with him curled into her like that whenever she'd be at the grocery store, or popping in and out of the little shops downtown, and maybe even in yoga class if he could really mold himself to her like a ferret or an extra-small orangutan.

Mrs. Thompson adjusted him like a mesh of oranges. She rolled him higher up. His ear brushed over the long raised scar on her chest, and his smooth cheek settled into the scar once she stopped sliding him up. He remembered her missing breast, the absence of mound and nipple. And he remembered the one full breast, burned into his mind or soul or wherever it was, he thought, that perfect images were implanted for the long haul. He pictured the long part of the nipple, the almost perfect circle, the few chill bumps, all this even though it was a lightening glimpse through glass, and he felt ashamed for spying on her, and he felt that a half-missing foot was a fitting punishment. But no, maybe not, but it was what he got. And he wished he could love Mrs. Thompson forever and let her know how beautiful she still was. And he marveled at what a good husband he would be to her, licking the scar along her chest and never commenting on absence in any form. Never commenting on a missing sock or the missing saltshaker from their honeymoon in the Bahamas. And, dammit, if Mr. Thompson didn't treat her well, he'd whoop his ass and swoop right in. And then again, would he need two socks now? Yes, he still would. And then again, could he court the radiant Mrs. Thompson when he and Julie were destined to spend a lifetime of ecstasy together regardless of whether she did or did not touch a penis during her time at the summer camp for the elite and wealthy? Tough to say, thought Keith.

Tough to say, because wasn't it true that he now was missing half a foot and in all likelihood, in all certainty he now supposed, would not make varsity as a freshman but would be lucky to come off the bench for the jv squad when they were heavily winning or heavily losing, and in such moments would he not get a roar of applause from the crowd when he hobbled out in his special shoe and had benchwarmers take it easy on him? Fuck that. Julie was all but gone. Julie was gone. Julie was totally gone. Gone like half of his foot blended in with the wet carnage of freshly halved grass. He was where he needed to be. Wrapped up in absence. Actually, filling in absence. His head nuzzling in perfectly where a breast had once been. He was where he needed to be, he thought. He was with the only person in the world who could possibly love him now. If only he could stop crying like some elementary schooler. If only he could stop crying and tell Mrs. Thompson exactly what she needed to hear in the world to feel as if life was always okay and she was still as beautiful as an angel descending to earth on a golden autumn morning in some European city, if, in fact, Mr. Thompson did not tell her such things, which he probably didn't, being the kind of guy who mailed his monthly check for lawn-mowing service instead of hand-delivering it, being the kind of guy who maybe worked late hours and maybe looked too long at his secretary's paired breasts, if he had a secretary, and so probably they would need each other now, Keith and Mrs. Thompson. Hopefully Mrs. Thompson could hold him like this forever, Keith thought. Hopefully she could hold him like this forever, or at least until he mustered the resolve to stop wailing like a non-freshman, but he probably couldn't stop his crying anytime soon.

Now his thinking was that she'd hold him only until the sirens arrived at her driveway, and then when the ambulance paused its scream and the paramedics darted to them, kneeling on the cut and uncut grass, she'd open her arms to release him to them. But he would cling to her still. He would cling to her with whatever strength he had left, his wet face burrowing into her chest, nuzzling into its warmth while his arms pressed into her sides and his fingers clenched her bathrobe. Eventually they'd pry him from her. Eventually they'd uncoil his fingers and straighten his body, placing him on a stretcher while working on what remained of his foot. They'd race him down Manor Drive, then turn on Main, passing his own house on the corner in three blocks, passing the yard with the unused tire swing where the cute girl from the private school sometimes sipped lemonade on the porch, and then at last passing the basketball court at the park three blocks south of the hospital. But for now, he clung to her. For now, he clung to her as the sirens raged louder and louder.

# III.

DEREK UPDEGRAFF

# AFTER SO MANY MILLENNIA OF BIRDS

Someone approaches Prometheus chained to the rock. The eagles have flown away and the wound has healed. Someone asks him, "Why are you chained to the rock like that?"

Prometheus is gray as rock, not arching his back, not lying anymore, just fused to cliffside. He says to Someone, "Ahhhh! I mean, you don't speak as birds!" He says, "I'm not sure why I'm here!" He says, "I don't remember why! But there's a reason for it!"

Someone says, "You don't have to scream while speaking." Someone says, "This has no meaning now. Let's get you down from here." Someone says, "Do you know your name?"

Prometheus says, "Perhaps my name is Lime?"

"Then your name is Lime," says Someone.

Someone unchains Lime, and Lime sits up from his rock bed, the skin of his back peeling off his body, stuck to the cliff.

"That's a different pain," says Lime.

"Yes, there are pains other than birds."

"That's good," Lime says.

"It is," says Someone.

Someone leaves Lime standing over his rock bed. Lime touches his toe to his back skin on the rock. Lime is still gray everywhere except his peeled back is red. Lime sees Someone walking away. Lime says, "Bye?"

Someone walks out of sight, slipping past another rock.

Lime is alone again. Having talked to Someone, he misses Someone. He thinks about curling down into his rock to wait for the morning birds. He hates the eagles while they tear at his liver, but then he misses them later in the long day, and at night he screams for them to come back when he should be sleeping.

But he doesn't join rock again. He tries out his legs instead. He walks down where Someone went even though Someone is long gone. He walks uneasy, like a newborn giraffe. He has to use his hands a lot at first. But after an hour or two he gets it. And then he strides. Oh, he strides.

He walks for half the day. He walks for the whole day. He comes to a town as the sky grays. He sees more someones. He says, "Ahhhh! I mean, hello!"

"Don't shout at me," says One.

"Forgive me," says Lime. "I am learning or relearning things. My talking has been screaming."

"Your back is bloody," says One. "I will wash it if you will take those loose rocks over there and stack them here."

"Here?"

"Yes, right there."

"I can stack those rocks," says Lime. "And do other things, I bet."

Lime makes a rock pile for One as tall as One.

Then One cleans Lime's back with a pitcher of water because the wound is slow to heal. They eat and drink at One's table, then stay together through the night.

At morning light, Lime takes a fork and makes quick stabs at his liver, pecking at the wound that has healed over after so many mornings. He stabs and stabs. He says, "This seems right."

"Is it?" says One.

"I thought so," Lime says.

One takes the fork and sets it on the table. One walks to the door and says, "Come. Let's make more rock piles instead."

# AUDITION

I'd asked my dad to drop me off a block away from the studio. Not because I was embarrassed by him or anything. We always got along great. I mean I wasn't a daddy's princess or anything. But we had fun. We joked when he wasn't stressed. But so I asked him to drop me off a block away because I needed to focus, to get in the zone. I wanted to visualize the day and how it was going to go down. Plus this was the nineties when everyone smoked, especially us dancers, especially when you're fifteen like I was then, and so I hopped out of my dad's car and kissed him on the cheek through his window, saying something like, "Bye, Daddy," and he would have said something like, "Knock 'em dead, sugar"—you know, something like he would have told a son going to football practice instead of his ballerina daughter off to an audition.

And I enjoyed that cigarette when I strolled down Linda Vista Road. This was back when SDB—that's San Diego Ballet—was over there instead of in Point Loma like now. So I had my duffle bag on me and I was in loose sweats because that's what you wear before getting your tights on but also because there were tons of creepers over in that area. And I remember just thinking that it was going to be my day, that after what happened at the SAB audition up there at DeFore's studio there was no way I wasn't going to dazzle the SFB reps. Karen had told me Lola herself was flying down for this call. And the fact that they were holding auditions for SFB at the studio I grew up in, well I just felt like fate was arranging it or something.

So inside I saw some of the girls I knew from classes. Karen gave five of us permission to audition, and then there was the regular cattle call. Girls from other San Diego studios. Girls from OC and LA. Some mid-state and Bay Area girls if they missed the SF call. Others who flew in from Washington or Colorado. Or even farther if they missed the Chicago or New York calls. So you know it was a big deal. And let me just skip ahead and let you know I nailed the audition. I mean you know I did because SFB is where I ended up for good after that summer program. And what I remember from the audition is that we did a typical barre with a company dancer leading it. But then when we went to center, Lola herself called out the combinations. And it was a surprise that she even flew down, but to have her run the audition, well, I just knew it was going to be a special day. And I tend to stay in the back, or I did back then, because I hadn't quite broken out of my shell, but Lola called me to the center in front of the panel. She said, "Number Sixteen, up front." And then she called out a 4-4 to the pianist, and I was unshakable.

And another thing from that day was glimpsing Amber in her dead shoes. Watching Amber out of the corner of my eye. Her trying to give it her all but knowing there's only so much you can do on dead shoes. There was this adagio combination she really struggled with. And I know that feeling because someone did it to me weeks before I did it to Amber. When I'd gone up to OC for the SAB audition, I knew I was on enemy turf. But still somehow I did the dumbest thing I could've done. I left my bag in the changing room when I was warming up alone in the hallway. And when I was done getting warm and went back to the changing room, I saw my bag unzipped, and my heart dropped and I was thinking, Stupid stupid stupid, and you know I'm about to say that my shoes were gone, and I looked around the room and the other girls looked oblivious, in their own zones, and I went into one of the bathrooms. And nothing. Then I went into another and, well, it smelled like shit and there were my toe shoes, in the damn toilet floating around with someone's shit. And that was that. I had some old shoes buried in my duffel. But they were dead, had dead shanks, just kept them as spares for easy stuff—you know, like you wouldn't want to do fouettes on them or anything. I was wearing Grishkos back then, loud shoes with a hard box, meaning you had to be good with your feet, know how to roll through your foot. But so anyway, my good toe shoes were in some girl's shit in the toilet, and you know I left them there. No way I'm reaching in for anything. So I had good soft shoes for the barre, and I made it past the barre, of course, and then there was still a crowd of us asked to go on to center, after girls were being yanked left and right during and after barre—Thanks, Number Twelve.

You're dismissed. Thanks, Thirty-eight. That's enough—the regular stuff. And then I had to wear my dead shoes for center, and I was in the twenty or so girls never yanked, but I never heard from SAB, and I was pretty limited with what I could do on those dead shoes. I did all the combos, kept pretty good lines, but I just didn't have the right support on those shanks. I just didn't pop that day, you know. And I'm not even sure who ruined my shoes. Don't know who saw me coming and was all—There's Claudette. I've heard of her, strong dancer—or something like that, and then saw her chance. Don't even know who did that, and I used to worry about it until things kept working out in my favor and then I didn't think about it much. Even now, recollecting it, I'm seeing how it might have been for the best.

So for the SF audition a couple weeks later my bag never left my side, and I was in my home element anyway. And there was this girl who had shown up, Amber, real talented, legs up to her armpits like me. New York style kind of, like she kept a straight back leg to prep for pirouette, but maybe the body type Lola would eat up and adjust to a West Coast style with a bent knee prep. And there were good girls all over the place. A few of them, you know, it's like, what are you doing here? Are you delusional? And they get yanked at barre. So of course there's tons of competition. And you can't sabotage everyone. And who would want to do that? You need to earn it. It needs to be earned. So I did it not just because Amber and I were similar and the opportunity presented itself. But it was more of a personality conflict type situation. The fact was, this girl was stuck up, like Dana Point stuck up. And she made the same mistake I did a few weeks earlier. She left her bag pushed up against the wall while she went off to stretch. And in that one tiny moment, my thinking was, Okay, they're only going to take a handful of girls from all the auditions combined, and if I'm one of those girls, I'll be hanging around the same few people all summer, and if I get taken and Amber gets taken and we somehow, somehow, end up as roommates for three months and possibly longer if the school courts us for the company, well, I'd just be in hell because that girl was obnoxious, toxic really, and here I had an opportunity to make sure she didn't follow me up north if I was San Francisco bound, which, as you know, I ended up being. So that was the split decision. And I walked by like a cat, slipped a hand in her bag, felt for the good toe shoes, and took them with me into a stall and lit them on fire with my lighter. Well, the whole things wouldn't light up, but I burned her ribbons down to nubs where she'd sewn them on and then I let the flame scorch over the rest of them for a while, but it started to smell and I got nervous and then I dumped them in the trash because they weren't actually on fire, just toasted, but useless without time to sew on new ribbons.

And, you know, I think back to when someone sabotaged me that one time, and I didn't end up in New York because of it, and now, as I said, I see I'm grateful in an odd way because of all that happened in SF instead. The years of solos. Not much corps work. The contemporary stuff choreographed for me. Dancing that mambo pas de deux with Miguel last year, for example, before I retired and he found out he was sick and took a turn for the worse. I mean, that was really special to me and so many other moments. And career-wise, well, Amber ended up at Pacific Northwest that summer, which was really more her speed anyway, and she had a quiet career in Toronto, I think, mostly in the corps I'm guessing, and that's how it would have worked out for her anyway.

The last thing I remember from that day is walking back down Linda Vista and crossing the street to meet my dad at Rose's, a little doughnut shop near the old studio. I ordered a lemon-filled and a raspberry-filled, because up to then it had been the standard one power bar and sixty-four ounces of water from wakeup till the afternoon audition. And so he was inside waiting for me as we'd planned, and he was reading the paper like people did pre-cell-phone era. And this I remember crisply. This I remember like it was yesterday and not nineteen years ago. He lowered his paper and stared at me while I stood above him. He studied me, and then he said, "Looks like you nailed it." I smiled. And he turned to no one in particular and said, "She's going places, this one. She's all confidence now, this one." And I said, "Thanks, Dad." And we ate doughnuts in silence, me devouring the raspberry first, him picking at his bear claw. And I think I already knew things would change soon. I think I knew then that I'd be on my way once spring had ended.

# ESTATE SALE

Driving home, Andrea makes out an Estate Sale sign at her neighborhood's entrance. She doesn't think much of it. Her mind drifts while the car heads home. Did she pack the kids' snacks in their front pouches? Yeah, she did. Would she want sex tonight? Maybe. She's ovulating and nostalgic. Just yesterday she had to go through Sandy's drawers again and box up more toddler clothes he's growing out of.

She passes more Estate Sale signs. She turns her turn. Another sign pops up, its arrow directing her to where she was already going. She veers onto Laredo, and there's the last sign, hammered into the lawn of her across-the-street neighbor.

She figures Mrs. Harrington must be dead. How did she not know this? How many days ago—weeks ago—did that happen? Her walkway roses have been looking a little dry recently. She kills the ignition, steps down from her mid-size, drifts across the street. She's drawn into her dead neighbor's house. Some woman says, "Welcome. Just opening up." Some man says, "Take a look around."

Andrea looks around. She cradles things in her palms: porcelain cups, figurines, antique school bells. She flips through records, fingers books. She studies church directories, watching the Harringtons age together each year until Mrs. Harrington's alone in the last few.

She sits in chairs, brushes fingers over a sewing machine. No room's off limits. She approaches the master bed. It's only a double. They would have had to touch a lot while sleeping. The closet is open. The clothes are tagged too. His clothes are gone, sold off or donated some years back. She pulls a dress off the hanger, sniffs musk, puts it back beside the peach jumpsuit Mrs. Harrington would wear when watering her roses. She moves to the dresser, opens one drawer, then another. The bottom drawer is full of lace. Doilies, she thinks. But she pulls out the fabric, and a camisole unfolds. A real sexy number. And so intricate. Floral stitching. Leaf-size holes to reveal slices of skin while the full sheen sections corralled breasts and buttocks. Each item seems to have been sewn by Mrs. Harrington, a collection of lingerie forged from tablecloths and doilies. Andrea clears out the drawer, gathering the softness in her arms.

In the living room the woman is greeting new passersby. The man is sitting at a card table with a little register. Andrea wonders if this man and woman are the Harringtons' children, here now to sell their parents' furniture, their mothers' knickknacks.

Andrea lays down the bundle of homemade lingerie on the table. She asks, "How much?"

The man says, "Oh my, is that? I don't think we marked that."

"How's twenty?" she asks. "Forty?" She coaxes two bills from her front pocket and floats them to his table. "They're good quality," she says, holding up a pair of panties stitched from doilies.

He's dazed, probably thinking of Mrs. Harrington in new light, perhaps gaining some insight into his recently passed mother.

Andrea corrals the mass of lingerie in her arms again. She gestures toward the bills on the table. She asks, "Good? Are we good?"

The man says, "Okay."

She's through the door and across the street. She's laying the items on her bed. She undresses and inches into the cream one with magnolias, careful not to tear any of the fine stitching. She fills it. It holds her well in the places it holds. She walks around her bedroom in Mrs. Harrington's homemade lingerie now hers. She's not encumbered. She moves like running water. She's thinking about her own mother, remarried, probably many years away from being alone. She's thinking about her children, what they'll make of her when they're clearing out her drawers one day, rummaging through her things with tags in hand. And she's thinking about her husband, what he'll think of the carefully stitched magnolias when she undresses tonight and pulls him to her.

She slides her clothes back on over Mrs. Harrington's lingerie. Then she puts the remaining items in her drawers, integrating them in with her own clothes, happy to have found such lovely things as these.

# THE BULL FROM KELP FOREST

"Fat girl/skinny guy is my favorite combination," he says to me. He's driving, and I'm in the passenger seat of his truck, our boards in the bed, bungee-corded down. We're about five minutes from the beach now, on surface streets, and when we were at that stoplight a minute ago, a fat girl and a skinny guy walked down the crosswalk, real sweet-like, his arm around her big waist, all proud, him in a tank top with those toothpick arms near those ham legs, and so Rob said that thing about the fat girl and the skinny guy being his favorite combo. And he's a jerk like that, but I'm just wondering where those two are heading in the dark, cold morning, with him in that tank top and her in her jean shorts. And now Rob says to me, "But there are other good ones too. Like rich girl/sketchy dude. Beefy guy/skinny chick. Short guy/tall girl. Like tree-tall girl with really short dude. That's a good one. But fat girl/skinny guy is hard to beat. It's a classic pairing."

Rob picked me up about a half-hour ago since my car's in the shop again. It was dark when he pulled up just after 4:30 am, and I was outside, not wanting to wake my wife and kids. I stood out on the curb for about ten minutes. The night/morning air was damp, and I missed how I used to get up early to do stuff like this. Get up early to surf in the morning before high school. Get up early in college to drive to the mountain and spend an entire weekday snowboarding, in both cases doing as much as we could to avoid crowds—me and Rob or another friend like him, and sometimes Dale was with us, but he could never quite keep up in big waves or on steep mountains—and if you don't have that impulse to rush down the tall, steep face of a wave or a mountain at sixteen or twenty-two, you're not going to get it later, because from what I've heard, people get more protective of their bodies as they get older, and I can't get that, but I think it's true for most, and I look at my life now, and I get up early to work my ass off, I get up early to tend to a crying twin if Sheila's conked out from feeding two kids at once or dealing with the diapers and everything, and so now on this morning I'm up early to run out into the freezing ocean where it's supposed to get up to ten feet, and I'm not thinking about anything but dropping in on the steepest waves I see, and I even like the idea of getting pummeled now and then if I miss the drop-in and get turned over and churn down under the water for a while before the tumult lets me up, and so there's no Dale today, just me and Rob like the best of our years before we ended up being our current twenty-nine-year-old selves.

We turn down the street that leads to the little parking lot by the pier, but you're not allowed to park in that lot anymore since they put up the signs, so Rob parks on the street across from the lot, where other rich folks like Rob live. But his parents' house is further up the hill with an ocean view, and he's living in the village part of town now anyway in a condo he probably doesn't pay for, but I don't ask about stuff like that because I don't care, but really I do care a bit and have always been a bit intrigued and envious of that inheritance after inheritance after inheritance passing on of imagined privilege and tangible wealth until someone down the line finally screws it up for the next in line.

But anyway we are on the street near the pier, and he pulls his truck to the curb, and he says, "Your car going to be ready before we meet up next week? I don't want to have to keep driving out there to get you. Too inland, you know." And he smirks. Because he'd keep driving out to get me, and he knows it. But he has to say jackass stuff like that. It's in his veins.

And I say, "You forgot rich boy/girl-of-the-day."

And he says, "What?"

"Your pairings," I say. "You forgot yourself. Rich boy and girl-of-the-day."

And we both laugh at that too. And I'm so glad not to be him. But we both know I'm a little envious. And then I realize I set myself up. And I'm waiting for him to come back with something. Poor kid/fill-in-the-blank. Scholarship kid/fill-in-the-blank. And what would he fill that blank in with?—because he doesn't know Sheila that well even though he was my best man at our wedding. And I'll knock him in the mouth, I swear, if he says something bad about Sheila, because I'm all about her right now even though I couldn't wait to get out of the house this morning. And he has no right to knock her because he was never with us when we dated at Pomona since he was up in Los Angeles. And screw those rich kids from our prep school anyway, especially Gary who I never see anymore, thank God, who asked me where I was going to college in our senior year and, when I said Pomona, was all, The good one or the bad one? Then I was all, What? And he repeated himself for the prep-kid-scholarship-boy who commuted from east of Richville, saying, The good one or the bad one? And then I got what he meant, and I said, Cal Poly. And he smirked and was all, Well, Sam will be up there too, nearby at Pomona College. And Rob was there, and he must have thought I needed saving because he said, He's going to be an engineer. Cal Poly Pomona's a good school for engineering. But I don't need rescuing, and I said—to Rob as much as to Gary—It's a good school for anything, you shits. But that's all beside the point because I'm waiting for Rob to say something about me and my girl, but he's still kind of getting a kick out of my girl-of-the-day comment, and once the laugh trails off he says, "Yeah, that's true." And then, "We should get some fish tacos after this for the long-ass drive back to your house."

He parks his truck and tosses his keys in the glove box. Then he pulls out a single spare key and puts it above the rear driver's-side tire after we get out of the truck. Then we grab the spring suits out of the back and towel-change them on. We toss our clothes and towels in the cab and push down the door locks, and then we grab our boards and cross the street. The asphalt is cold and newly smoothed, but I still step lightly out of habit from slamming my heel down on sharp pebbles too many times throughout the years, which isn't bad if you're already done for the day but you don't want to prick your feet up before you've even been out in the water, so I'm light on the balls of my feet like a chick in heels or some graceful animal just for a minute as we cross the road. And then we're on the sidewalk heading to the staircase. The concrete is even colder and harder than the asphalt, and there are sand pieces strewn here and there that start to stick to the bottoms of my feet. And then we're bouncing down the concrete staircase, then we're on the cold soft sand, then we're galloping onto the wet sand, and then there we are, darting, feet and legs crushing the water until we're at our knees, and we jump on our boards, chest and fiberglass meeting horizontally, and we're skimming for a few feet, side-by-side, like brothers, like twins even but with different hair color, and then, before our momentum slows, we start to paddle, and our hands and arms break the water and scoop back around, and white water rumbles toward us as waves break and rush to the shore, and we hit the first few small ones head on and the cold water licks face and neck and collects in hair, and it exhilarates, and it's the exact coldness you need to finish waking you up and keep you sharp for what's to come since the waves are tall today, and as we keep paddling out and the broken waves ahead of us are large and unruly we start to duck-dive the rest of the way, pushing the front of the board beneath the water a few feet down, then following under with our heads and bodies while a foot shoves the back part of the board beneath the water too, and for a few seconds I'm under and Rob's under and our boards are held under by hands, then feet, and the mass of white water thunders over us and doesn't push us back to the shore since we're good at duck-diving and are far enough under the water that it passes over us and we pop up on the backside of the wave with the tip of the board breaking the water first and then our heads and shoulders following, and the moment we are back on top of the water lying on our boards we are furiously paddling again, and again a mass of white water rumbles toward us, and again we duck-dive under a broken, charging wave, and then another, and then under a wave still breaking, and then we are out in the clearing of calm water, in the line-up past the breaking point, and we sit up on our boards, our legs on each side while our boards are a foot under water, and I splash water on my face and slick my hair back with my hands.

In the line-up it's just me and Rob, so we won't be competing for waves until others start showing up, and the sun is almost out at this point, but it's still mostly a dark, dark gray. We're usually pretty quiet with each other once we're out on the water. But sometimes we get to talking. But then we have to take long pauses whenever a set comes in because we would rather drop in on the next wave instead of talk about anything. I think about asking him how he's doing. But he's always fine. Mr. Fortunate. Mr. Single-Without-Kids. Mr. Rich-Boy-Grown-Up who doesn't have to worry about the things I worry about. But he's always been my best friend, and I do love the jackass, and there's a set approaching, so instead of asking him anything, I reach out for one of the floating seaweed pieces, and I rip off the big leaf and hold on to the bulbous part. They're about the size of a golf ball but smaller and ovaler, more oval-like I mean, and I hold it between my thumb and two fingers and pinch down on it and the little thing rockets out of my hand, shooting out from the slime and pressure, and it smacks him in the cheek and drops to the water, and I laugh and he laughs, and I turn my board around and start paddling to the shore as the first of this set keeps approaching, and I'm paddling hard now, and I'm angling just right as I'm shooting forward with my paddling and this wave slowly building under and behind and in front, and it's taking shape, and all this space opens up in front of me, and the tide is low so this happens pretty quickly, and I'm staring down a growing wall of water, but I'm just in the perfect place and angled just enough, and I paddle and paddle because I'm on a shortboard, six-foot-six, none of that longboard nonsense, and so I paddle and paddle because on a shortboard you really have to get in there before you pop up, and now I'm in there, and I pop up, pressing my chest up, my hands on the rails, then my feet sliding beneath my body and my hands in the air to my side once I'm standing, and this is a movement that takes a half-second to do when you know what you're doing, and I'm up, and I ride regular with my left foot forward, and Rob rides goofy with his right foot forward, and Dale—well I don't remember how Dale rides because I don't see him up very often, just see him getting pummeled on the inside or see him sitting outside in the line-up chatting about this or that, too afraid to drop in on anything on big days like this one—and so I'm there dropping into the first one of the day, and I take it to my right because that's the way it's breaking there at that spot. So I'm about to face the wave, which is my favorite way to be, and I drop in and I'm about three or four feet down the thing, angling just right, and I've got about another six feet below me as the water is being sucked up from down there, sucked up and racing up this face, and I've got to tell you that this is about one of the best feelings in the world because it's all so fast, and if you see it from the shoreline, from the outsider's perspective, it might not seem like much, but from my view, from our view when we do this, man, those few feet below me seem like a building's length, and I'm bending my legs just enough, but my style is to stay kind of straight up still, but I'm bending my knees a little, and I shoot down those last few feet, and I turn hard toward the wave, and I head back toward it before turning back a little bit, and now we're in sync, me and the wave, and we're unfolding at the same rate, and it's over my head three or four feet as it keeps shooting me to my right, angling me down as more and more of its length turns to white foam, but I'm in the sweet spot the whole time, and it's getting smaller and smaller as we're angling in the shore's direction, and it's about at my head now, and normally I'd do a little move or two now, pop up for a floater or something, but this is my first one of the day, and I'm just appreciating being out, so I just cruise on this thing as it loses its power, as so much water that was making this wave is breaking away from it and spreading out into other parts of the ocean until it's only knee-high now, and the water is only a few feet deep, and I'm pumping the front of the board up and down to keep on the wave, and then it's done, and I belly flop off because, Why not?—it's early and cold and I'm happy to be here, and then I'm on my feet in a couple feet of water, and I'm horizontally on my board and paddling back out into the line-up, duck-diving duck-diving duck-diving, and now my arms are feeling the sting a bit, but I'm in the line-up and I catch my breath, and I look around to see where Rob is.

Rob must have caught one of the waves after me because now he's paddling back out, about twenty feet away, and he pops out of the back of a wave he's just duck-dived, and now he's paddling toward me, and now he's here next to me. And he sits up on his board and splashes his face with water like I do, and he reaches for some floating seaweed, pulls off a little floater ball from one of the leaves, and shoots the thing at me like I did to him. The seaweed ball plinks my chest, bouncing off my wetsuit and hitting the water. I pick it up and plink it back at him, and it hits his shoulder and drops again. We've been doing this since high school, hitting each other with these little seaweed bulbs. It's kind of a fun way to pass the time, and they feel neat in your hands, and sometimes when you squeeze too hard when you're trying to shoot it out, the thing caves in and makes a loud popping sound.

We stop shooting the seaweed bulbs, and things are quiet out in the line-up. The sky is still more dark than light, but it's no problem seeing everything. Probably in twenty minutes or so when the light has really spread out everywhere, more surfers will show up, and our little spot will start to crowd, and we'll have to start competing for the waves.

"It's pretty warm now," I say, pushing my hands back and forth in the water in front of me.

"Yeah," says Rob. "It's nice. It should be a good spring this year. Some good storms for us."

"Yeah, that's good," I say, and I'm about to say something about hoping to find more time to come out here more often, but there's another set coming, and this time Rob is paddling for the first one, and I watch as he paddles past me on top of the flowing water that is building into a wave, and he's darting away now, and the wave is big and building up quickly, and I half-see him drop in and disappear as the back of his wave climbs up, but really I'm more focused on the other bumps of water coming toward me, the second and third waves of the set building up in the distance. And the third looks like the biggest of the bunch. And it's really building fast, and I have to paddle out farther because if I stay where I am, the thing would break on me and I'd miss it, so I paddle out farther real quick, and then I turn my board and body quickly and redirect myself to angle toward the shore, and just like that I paddle only one or two strokes and this monster builds so fast and sucks me in, and I push down, and I'm kind of too far to the top and should be more in the middle as it's building, but I'm high at top, and I pop up early and force myself down, and I'm staring down what has to be fifteen feet of face, and I have a quick second where I can still pull out, but there's no way I'm doing that, and I feel the lip pushing me in, and I crouch down a bit and hold onto my rail with my right hand to steady my board, and I get hurled forward, and I'm off the wave now. I'm in front of the wave because it spit me forward since I was too high, and I am in the middle of the air, and there is this mass of breaking water behind me, as tall as a house, and I land flat on the water fifteen feet below, but I didn't angle enough, and the wave breaks down right where I am, and I take a good breath of air because I know what's coming, and the breaking white water flings me upward after I'd just touched down, and then I fall back down again into the mass of broken, rushing water, and I'm pulled under the wave and start to get churned about, like I'm in some massive washing machine, and I'm getting rolled over and over, and the whole time I'm as calm as a fish when someone like Dale would be freaking out and sucking in water, and my mouth is tight, and I'm tumbling and tumbling until finally the wave has moved on, and I'm about four or five feet underwater in a calm section between waves, and now I swim to the top and take a breath, and I pull my board over to me by the leash strapped to my ankle, and I get back on horizontally, face the direction of the line-up, and paddle and duck-dive, paddle and duck-dive, until I am back out in the line-up.

Rob is there. And he says, "That looked fun."

"You saw that?" I say. "It's too bad. It was big."

"You were too far in."

"I know. But I had to try. How was your wave?"

"Good. Better than my first."

We're quiet again and looking out for the next set. And as if by instinct, we each reach for some seaweed and start pulling the leaves off the little floaters. And we've each got a few of the oval bulbs in our hands. And we fire them at each other, and they miss or else they clink off our chests or arms. And then another set approaches in the distance, slowly rolling toward us, and because it's still more gray than light, and because we still have the line-up to ourselves and others will be encroaching soon, we turn around and prepare to paddle to where we need to be to catch these next ones. And as Rob kind of whips around the point of his board and spins himself while still sitting on it, he's facing me, and I have the last seaweed bulb in my hand, so I squeeze it and fire it at his face like we do, and right then he yawns, but I've already started swinging my board around, and I'm already horizontal now and paddling for the first wave in the set, and I'm paddling forward—but didn't he just yawn? I'm thinking—and I look over my shoulder while the wave is building beneath me and hurrying me along, and I see him yawning in slow motion, and the bulb I shot goes right in his mouth—the little thing was speeding—and I laugh while I'm about to drop in—but then I wonder if he's choking, or did he spit the thing out okay, and I'm still lying on my board about to pop up, and I still have time to pull out and paddle back to check, but I'm thinking, No, I'm sure he's fine. But didn't I hear choking, and I'm thinking, No, that wasn't choking. That was the sound of this wave. And then I'm up and racing down the face of this one, and I'm caught up in it, in the moment. I'm feeling free, and I'm just standing and riding again. No tricks today. Just old school cruising. And this is another big one. It's solid and dangerous, but I'm really calm on it. I'm just riding this thing out. I'm not in control. I'm being taken. And what could I do anyway? And the spray hits my face. And it's so cold and really reminds me about living. And more spray hits my face. And sometimes things just come out of nowhere.

A different friend's dad once told us a story about a guy on the back of a garbage truck. Back when garbage trucks had a driver and a guy or two hanging on the back who would hop off and throw the garbage in the back at each house stop. Not like now where a mechanical arm does it. So my friend's dad and his friends are driving in a convertible, and they're young, just cruising, hanging out, but they're behind a garbage truck. And the trash pick-up guy hanging on the back spits this loogie, a real big nasty one, and my friend's dad's friend in the passenger seat of the convertible, well he yawns and stretches his arms and kind of stands up a little, and because he stands up a little, his head is higher than the windshield, and the garbage man's loogie goes right into the guy's mouth. Just like that. Out of nowhere. And the way my friend's dad tells it, the guy was pissed and disgusted and downright shocked. It was the shock of it, having someone else's spit and mucus ball land right in your mouth like that. And I'm thinking about that story as this wave is fizzling out near the shore because I'm sure Rob was super shocked by the slimy piece of sea bulb landing in his rich mouth, which isn't as bad as a loogie anyway. And maybe because he had to spit the thing out I caused him to miss his wave. Oh, for shame, if I caused such a thing.

And I hop off my board into shoulder-high water, and my feet bounce off the sand, and I pull myself back on my board, lying horizontally, getting ready to duck-dive my way back into the line-up, to laugh a bit at Rob, but there's his board about thirty feet ahead of me, between me and the line-up, and it's bouncing around in the white water of a dying but still fierce wave, and the board wants to come toward me, but its leash pulls it tight and keeps it in check, and I'm waiting to see Rob's face and hands and shoulders pop out of the water somewhere, and I'm waiting for that gasp of air—like when we would train ourselves to hold our breaths longer underwater by walking along the bottom of his pool while cradling a cinder block to keep us down, and then when our lungs burned for air and it seemed, after minutes, like we couldn't handle another second, we'd let go of the cinder block and float slowly to the surface, and then we'd gasp gasp gasp and suck and eat the air. I'm waiting for that gasp from Rob now, but I know it's not coming. And I know that choking sounds like choking and not a wave.

And then Rob's body does pop up, but it's his back with his head still under, and in his black wetsuit his rounded back poking through the water looks like a rock or a seal head because he's still at least twenty feet away, and I realize I've been kind of paralyzed in my mind while I was surfing and probably knew my friend was choking—or did I not know that?—but now I'm finally clear-headed, and I'm paddling over to the bobbing lump. I'm furiously paddling over to the bobbing lump. And my arms are burning, but man, I'm racing across the water so fast, and I get to my friend before the next wave comes, and I flip him over, and he's pale in the skin and purple in the lips and eyes, and I undo his leash from his ankle so his board can dart to the shore, and I maneuver him onto my board, adjusting him until he's straight on his back. And I steady the board while holding it and floating next to it, and as the next rush of white water comes, I get between the board and the wave, and I throw my back into it to take the hit, and then I push the board forward and hold my friend's feet and the back of my board as the wave takes them and then takes me kicking behind while holding board and friend together, and we ride the wave all the way to the sand, me dragging behind, and there are people on the beach since the light is coming through the gray. They are getting ready to go out and surf, but now they see Rob on the board and me dragging the board across the wet, firming sand until we're out of the water's lick, and I'm beating down on his chest, and I'm craning my finger throughout his mouth, craning it all around in there trying to dislodge and scoop out the seaweed bulb that he must have— probably?—swallowed, and I tilt his neck back and put my hand under there like he's my girl, and I lock my lips on his and blow in air like I was taught way back when we were junior lifeguards together for three summers, and then I go back to working on his chest, really hammering my palms down, and there's the crack of a rib or two, but still I hammer hammer hammer, and right when I'm about to try for more air, the damn bulb shoots out of his mouth and over my head, and then he's spitting up water and coughing, and I roll him to his side, and there are way more people around us than I thought, a whole crowd really, and up in the parking lot there are the flashing lights of an ambulance, and there are murmurings around me. Maybe something about a hero, but my mind is too foggy again to process the din.

The paramedics take him off my board and put him onto their gurney. Rob hasn't said a word. He's coughing lightly and one of the medics is attending to him. Another one is asking me questions while we're all kind of jogging across the sand in our cluster. Two carrying the gurney, one talking to me while we're moving. And I'm thinking, Aren't they supposed to come in pairs, not trios? And then I say something about finding him bobbing around in the water, and then doing CPR. I say he must have swallowed some seaweed because a bulb shot out during CPR, and I can see Rob's eyes locked on me while he's strapped down, but he's not talking, and I can't quite tell what, if anything, is going on behind those eyes. Can't tell if that glazed look means he's doing okay in there or if he has some brain issue. And just as soon as the medics come, they're off, and I've given them Rob's name and info, and they tell me what hospital they're rushing him to, and I say I'll be right behind them.

But before I leave, I walk back toward the water's edge to collect my board. It has a few new dings, but it will work fine. I tuck it under my arm, and I'm about to walk to Rob's truck to drive to the hospital or maybe just home, maybe just crawl in bed with Sheila before the bulk of the day hits, nuzzle in beside her before I relay the mishap, but then I remember Rob's board too. And it isn't to the left. But there to the right it's being pushed to the sand, then pulled back to the ocean, then pushed to the sand again. I get it and tuck it under my other arm. I guess the crowd of people is in the water now. It is definitely morning now. The best breaking spot that had been mine and Rob's is already muddled. All those late risers who think they're early risers out there fighting for position in the line-up. We would still be out there too if this hadn't happened. We would be out there, but we'd know the best rides had passed before the others spoiled it. And I bungee-cord our boards in the bed of the truck, and as I'm reaching for the key left on top of his tire, and as I'm unlocking the driver's door and getting in and staying in my wetsuit while the last bit of ocean in it soaks the seat—while all that is happening I'm thinking about that sweet chubby girl and her valiantly thin guy, and I'm wishing them the best, and thinking of them being happy together, and their warmth makes me think maybe we're not all so bad, not all bad as we're slow to react to things, or sometimes choose to let others fend for themselves for a while before stepping in and helping out, and so all I can do right now is drive forward, move on in this truck I'll get to borrow until my car gets fixed or maybe longer.

DEREK UPDEGRAFF

IV.

DEREK UPDEGRAFF

# AT THE DOG PARK

The crazy lady with the Doberman's back, over by the front gate asking her same question: "Your dog have balls? Hey, does that dog have balls?" Her dog has balls, and he's mean and couldn't care less about what she says. Yesterday I saw him running all around the parking lot with his leash on before chasing a jogger. She's there calling out and he doesn't respond to nothing. I hoped he'd get hit by a car or run off into the mountain, but then again it's not the dog's fault he's such an asshole.

"None of these dogs in here have balls," I shout back.

"What!" she says.

I walk closer to the gate. "No balls. Only your dog has balls. That sign you're standing by, it says, 'No balls.'"

"It doesn't say, 'No balls.'"

"Read it. Dogs need to be spayed or neutered. That means no balls for that guy there."

She lifts the latch and comes in anyway. "It doesn't say that." Her dog wastes no time, runs away from her with his leash on and zeros in on something called a Whoodle. The pretty boy owner told me it was a cross between a Poodle and something else, some small breed that starts with a W. You've got a Shepsky, he told me. German Shepherd and Husky mix, right? And I said he's just a mutt, no fancy hybrid, just a mutt from the shelter.

I don't worry about my dog in here because he can take care of himself. And he listens. I hike off leash in the mountain, and when he runs off, I give him time, then call him back, and Bam! he's there, right by me on the trail again.

But this Doberman and his dangling balls zeroed in on that boy's Whoodle, and the Whoodle's a hyper thing, thinks the Dobie wants to play. It sticks its ass in the air and lowers its head all playful, its tail wagging like crazy, but the Dobie's tail isn't wagging, and its chest puffs out and it bumps the Whoodle's side, and just like that the Dobie spins the Whoodle to mount it, but the Whoodle flips on its back in submission, so instead of doggie style the Dobie is all up on this dog in the missionary position, and the Whoodle's owner is screaming like crazy from twenty feet away, yelling for the dog to stop humping him, that he's a boy anyway, and to please get your dog off, Ma'am!

The crazy lady's oblivious, filling her water bottle at the drinking fountain, and Whoodle boy won't dare get closer, so I go over there and yank the Dobie off the pup, and he bites my arm hard, and I'm about to punch it in the head when my mutt's right there biting its neck. Then when my arm's out, he wrestles the Dobie down and clamps down on his balls, dragging the poor bastard by his coin purse, deflating any envy.

# CINDER

The girl with broad shoulders in the powder blue Cinderella gown neared a turnstile outside Disneyland. The girl was not so much a girl but a thirty-nine-year-old accountant named Denise. But Denise felt like a young girl whenever she inched into one of her princess gowns. She has three now, each one hand-stitched by a client who owns an alteration shop. If Denise has another good year, she'll get sized up for a blue and yellow Snow White gown to make it four. One day she'd like a closet full of gowns in her otherwise common house with common furniture and common household things. And now outside Disneyland, alone but scheduled to meet someone, a guy named Cliff, she still felt like a young girl, all befuddled with first-date jitters while the silk—Is it silk? she thought—or other such smooth fabric hugged her round muscular body so nicely.

Ever since she got into dressing up like princesses again, she preferred going to Disneyland in October. The locals all know that the late-fall to early-spring months are the best at Disneyland, to avoid too many tourists, except at Christmastime, when that's impossible. But then again there are always too many tourists all year long, but really the reason to go in late fall and winter is to avoid the heat and sweat while standing in line for sixty minutes for Snow White's Scary Adventure or Peter Pan's Flight, when really a twenty-minute wait seems more appropriate for those short but still-so-incredible rides. And Denise was glad that the early-October air was in the mild 60s as she approached the park, now at about 6:30 pm, because in this coolness she could rock her Cinderella gown with shoulders out and smooth armpits visible when going "yay" on a ride with arms up without too much fear of sweat building.

She showed her annual pass to the turnstile cast member. Cast member, even for the turnstile guy or gal, since Disneyland favors "cast member" over unmagical titles like "employee" or "turnstile guy." Denise preferred it that way too, all magical.

The cast member playing her turnstile guy scanned her annual pass, and when her name popped up, he said, "Welcome, Princess Denise." And the turnstile cast members all tend to say that to her even when she's not in a princess dress, but it was particularly nice to hear it today when she looked the part. If only she could always wear one of her princess dresses when she went to Disneyland, but they had rules about dressing up like that—only in the Halloween season—except for the little kids, who could dress up all year long, even in cheap Walmart dresses. So throughout October Denise would frequent Disneyland as often as she could after work, changing into a princess gown in the parking structure before boarding the tram. As soon as the Halloween season passed, she pulled out her gowns only on the occasional weekend, mostly wearing them around her house, skipping across the living-room carpet after carefully sliding into a gown, then humming a melody with her makeup more vivid than usual. She'd sometimes even spend a Saturday at the beauty salon getting her hair and nails done, and then once home she'd put on her Cinderella, Aurora, or Belle gown, having a fun time while Little Bruno, her basset-hound/beagle mix, pranced alongside her while she dropped a Pup-Peroni doggy treat every few steps. She used to wear her gowns in her backyard also, on mild days when the grass was dry and the ground firm, but she stopped frolicking in her backyard in princess garb ever since that one day when she caught sight of the neighbor boy spying on her, peering over the top of the wooden fence while standing on something, probably snickering, probably thinking how silly she looked. But all she really saw was his wide wide eyes staring at her as she skipped in a circle, his wide wide eyes beneath his baseball cap with something like an eagle or a falcon on it, some sports logo with an orange flame in the background, and she thought about keeping on with her routine and letting him watch her, but she couldn't stand not knowing what he thought of her—freakish or delightful—and so she shuffled into the house and stopped wearing her gowns in the backyard.

Inside the park, powder blue Cinderella gown hugging her hips, hair in a bun, she headed straight toward the iconic Fantasyland Castle. That was where she had told Cliff to meet her.

She'd met Cliff through an online dating site, one of the respectable ones she'd use now and again, and she always insisted on communicating through e-mail exchanges for at least one month before seeing a potential suitor in person. And Cliff had written that that was a smart policy of hers, and for weeks now they'd been writing each other, discussing things like work—her being an accountant, him being a history teacher at Jefferson High, her alma mater's rival some decades ago. "Go Roos!" she wrote in one of her e-mails. "Go Grizzlies!" he joked back. And they discussed things like their hopes and dreams, and their hobbies, and their pets—her owning Little Bruno, him owning a pair of cats named Lewis and Clark. He wrote once that he sometimes liked to tell people his cats' names were Clark and Lewis, just to see if they'd get it. She wrote "LOL" to that. And sometimes she wrote things like, "How are your little fur babies today?" and "Do your little adventurers get excited when you come home? My little fur baby gets so happy whenever I get back from work."

And then after a few weeks she wrote that they should meet, suggesting a date at Disneyland now that Halloween season had arrived, now that the Haunted Mansion would be decorated with fun Jack Skellington stuff, suggesting too that wouldn't it be fun to dress up even, now that it's October, to dress up, just for fun, when they had their first date to add to the magic. And he wrote back, "Gosh, that DOES sound fun!" and she wrote back, "Neat!!! i am SO Excited!!!" And she let him know that she would be dressed up in a nice Cinderella gown that a friend had once made for her, just for fun, and did he think he could, if it wasn't too much trouble, perhaps find a well-made Prince Charming outfit, one of good quality from a nice rental place. "If it's not too much trouble," she wrote, "only if it's not TOO much trouble???"

And Cliff had found a good-quality Prince Charming outfit and e-mailed Denise a picture of it, a picture of it on its hanger, though she had wished he'd sent one with him in it. And Cliff had purchased a ticket to Disneyland for the day of their date since he didn't have an annual pass like she did. And she appreciated the effort he was putting into this first magical date of theirs, renting the outfit, buying the ticket, agreeing to meet in front of the Fantasyland Castle instead of walking into the park together.

On her way to the castle, Denise didn't notice the quaint details of Disneyland she loved so much, the charm of the little shops in Main

Street, U.S.A. and the like. She just headed toward the castle, not really noticing the Halloween costumes the kids and adults were wearing, not thinking about how nice it was to be able to wear a princess gown and not have everyone staring like she was an oddball or something. She walked steadily so as not to break a sweat. And the air was not hot or cold. She didn't notice air. Or temperature. She wore long white gloves that stretched to her elbow, and her shoulders were puffed in fabric, and her biceps were visible between elbow and shoulder, and her gown hung perfectly for her height, so that it reached her heels without dragging on the ground, and her neck was bare, of course, and the top line of her breasts was visible, in a tasteful way. And the skin that was covered and the skin that was exposed felt the same to her, not warm but something just below warm, something mild, something comfortable.

When she neared the castle, she stopped short of the drawbridge and took it all in. So beautiful, she thought, so wonderful that this exists for us to appreciate. And it wasn't too crowded. And she looked around and couldn't see Cliff anywhere, couldn't see Prince Charming anywhere. And she thought that it was only proper for him to approach her, so she kept walking forward until she reached the bridge—their designated meeting place—and she took her phone out of her purse and glanced at the time—6:53—and then she put her phone away, and she stood in the center of the bridge, but people were steadily passing through in each direction, so she stepped toward the side and looked over the railing and into the water, where ducks were swimming and where a cute little statue of Snow White and the dwarfs stood on the opposite bank, and then she felt a hand on the puff of her shoulder, and she turned and saw Cliff's stately golden sash across his chest before she took in the rest of him— the golden shoulder pads with golden tassels, the maroon pants with a golden stripe crawling up each leg.

They faced each other, staring into eyes but also glancing up and down, him absorbing the gown, her absorbing his princely attire. He was fifty-two, and his face reflected his age, wrinkles here and there, and his hair reflected his age, black hair now showing tufts of gray, and he looked just like his photos, and how refreshing it was that he looked just like the pictures he'd sent her, and that he hadn't lied about his age like some of the others, and really, she thought, his few wrinkles added a distinguished quality. He was very distinguished, indeed, she kept thinking.

"You look beautiful," Cliff said. "That is a nice gown. Looks professional. I mean the quality. It looks professionally made."

"Thank you," said Denise. "It's my favorite one. And you look quite handsome. Very distinguished. And also so princely."

"You have others?"

"Others?" Denise said.

"Other gowns. You said this was your favorite. You have more?"

"A few others. I guess it's silly. I didn't mean to let that slip out just yet."

"No. No," said Cliff. "I think it's lovely. I think it's great. I'd love to see the others someday too. You look lovely. I mean, you are lovely. I hope that's okay for me to say."

And Denise smiled and bit back a squeal and said, "Thank you. Yes, definitely."

And Cliff in his Prince Charming garb reached out a bent arm and asked, "Shall we, my lady?"

And Denise put her arm through his and said, "Yes, my dear sir."

And the two of them walked arm-and-arm through the castle and into Fantasyland, and they veered right toward Peter Pan's Flight, and they waited in line for about twenty minutes, talking as good friends and potentially more, talking to each other in the same easy way they had been in their e-mail exchanges for the past few weeks, and then they rode Peter Pan's Flight and had fun like children, smiling and laughing and soaking in the magic, and then they rode Mr. Toad's Wild Ride and Snow White's Scary Adventure and Pinocchio's Daring Journey and even hoisted themselves up onto side-by-side horses on the King Arthur Carrousel. Then they both decided to pass on the Mad Tea Party because they each said that the spinning teacups made them too dizzy, but they did ride Alice in Wonderland, of course, and then they backtracked to ride Dumbo the Flying Elephant even though Cliff was afraid of heights, as he had just then confided to her, and Denise said, "Only if you're up for it," and Cliff said, "I'm up for it. Let's give it a try," and Denise thought that was so sweet of him to brave the Dumbo ride for her since she had told him it was one of her favorites. And on the ride, when the Dumbo they were sitting in had reached its full height in the air, looping around in a wide circle so they could see so much of the park below, she flung her arms in the air unabashedly and smiled wide, and though she did not let out any noise, in her head she was saying, Wee! Wee! Wee!

After the Dumbo ride, Cliff asked if they should get a bite to eat or head over to another land. Denise said that she was too excited to eat, that maybe they could eat later, perhaps catch a late dinner at the Village Haus Restaurant before staking out a good spot to see the parade and fireworks, if that was okay with him.

And he felt the same way and said, "How about the Haunted Mansion?"

And she said, "Yes, definitely, and we can swing by Pirates on the way. And then after Pirates and the Mansion we can do Splash Mountain and then Winnie the Pooh and then circle back for Big Thunder."

They waited in line for Pirates of the Caribbean, and they chatted about their pets Bruno and Lewis and Clark, and then they got in their boat and sat in a row beside a couple dressed as Danny and Sandy from *Grease*, all slicked out in 50s gear, and Denise thought to herself, What a cute couple, and then she thought to herself, We are a couple.

The wait for the Haunted Mansion was the longest because of the seasonal Jack Skellington decorations. Denise didn't really mind slow lines at Disneyland because she liked absorbing the atmosphere. She loved everything about the place. Especially the trees.

"Don't you love these trees," she said to Cliff. "They're so old." And she worried then that he might think that was a jab at his age, and so she added, "And they're still so vibrant and lively even though they're mature and sturdy."

And he said, "They are beautiful. But not as beautiful as you."

She blushed and looked from his face to an old magnolia tree stretching high up and over so many of the folks waiting in line. "That's sweet," she said. "But look at that magnolia's flowers. They look like velvet or silk or just soft snow. Amazing. I just love it here."

"And I love being here with you," said Cliff.

And for the first time that day, Cliff took Denise's hand in hers and squeezed it. And she shivered like a middle-school girl and squeezed his hand back.

They zigzagged through the line, holding hands, looking like so many of the other couples brought to Disneyland for their own date night. And they inched forward toward the Haunted Mansion, commenting on other trees, and on the hedges and all of the fine landscaping in general, and commenting too on the little details that made the wait in line a pleasurable experience, like the headstones lining the path with clever epitaphs like DEAR DEPARTED BROTHER DAVE HE CHASED A BEAR INTO A CAVE.

In front of them, a couple dressed as a wolf and Little Red Riding Hood stood while leaning into each other. Another couple wearing matching Mickey and Minnie t-shirts with "His" and "Hers" printed on them groped each other whenever the line came to a halt. They were young teenagers, and Denise looked around for their parents before she realized they probably wouldn't be there.

The line moved toward the side of the Haunted Mansion, and Denise and Cliff still squeezed each other's hands. Denise had a toothbrush, travel-sized toothpaste, and breath mints in her purse for the fireworks' kiss later in the evening. She had it all planned out: ride rides, eat a light dinner, excuse herself to the restroom and brush teeth and pop in breath mints—and pee if necessary (actually, probably pee no matter what, squeeze out what she could, to feel airless and dainty when kissing during Fireworks Spectacular)—then watch parade, and then watch fireworks and wait for him to initiate kiss, but if he doesn't, be bold, Denise, she was telling herself, so bold that you take him in your arms and plant one on him while the night sky and Fantasyland Castle are lit up and reflecting off your gown and his Prince Charming shoulder tassels.

Before she knew it, they were being ushered into the Haunted Mansion, guided into the glorious building. And they stood with their group in the room that felt like an elevator moving while the walls lengthened and the paintings grew upward, revealing hidden scenes beneath each portrait, like the young girl holding a parasol who, as the image stretches, is shown to be standing on a tightrope above a pool of water with an alligator waiting beneath her, his jaws opened wide.

After leaving the room with the stretching portraits, they walked through the long hallway toward the ride, the hallway filled with pictures whose images shift on their own. A young woman morphs into a snake-haired gorgon like Medusa. A young man ages into a skeleton, but his eyes stay pristine even after his head is a skull. And a ship at sea transforms into a wreckage with tattered sails. Along with these classic Haunted Mansion fixtures, decorations from *The Nightmare before Christmas* had been placed here and there, showing Jack Skellington and Sally the sweet rag doll and the others. And each year Disneyland added new seasonal features and changed things around. She couldn't wait to see how things were staged on the ride this year.

At the end of the hallway, she stepped onto the moving walkway and then climbed into the ride's passenger car—the "Doom Buggy," the recorded voice said ghoulishly. Cliff leaped in next to her, and the pair was alone in the two-seater car. They were gliding along the ride's pathway, and all of the fantastic scenes were ahead of them. The ballroom and the graveyard were her favorites. And then in the grayness while their passenger car scooted along its track, away from the line they were in, ascending slowly into the first magical scene, Denise felt Cliff's hand rest on her thigh, and he squeezed her thigh, and Denise thought that maybe now he would lean in for a kiss, and it's not where she envisioned it happening, but she was ready to kiss him there, in the Haunted Mansion, because that's a sweet first-kiss story too, though not as magical as fireworks, but still romantic, she guessed, in its own seasonal way. But he did not lean in for a kiss. He looked at her, and she stared at him, and with their bodies facing forward and their heads turned inward, eyes seeming to grasp at some shared understanding, he kept squeezing her thigh, and then another hand gathered the gown at its opening, bundling the fabric from ankles to lap so that now her stockings were exposed from foot to thigh, and a hand slid up her inner thigh, and just before it closed in on its destination, she blocked it with a free hand, intertwining her own fingers with its, holding it there while pressed against her flushed thigh. And she said to him, "Not here, okay?" And he stayed silent while still staring at her, and she couldn't read him. And then he pulled out their locked hands from beneath her gown, and he placed her hand in his lap, and he started moving her hand around on the outside of his pants, and he whispered, "Let's at least do this."

And Denise let him guide her hand for a moment, for a second, before she pulled it back to herself and said to him again, "Not here. Not like this, okay?"

And he said to her, still staring at her, "You've got to be fucking kidding me." And his voice was not raised, it was even, but it sounded loud in the passenger car, where they were supposed to be quiet, where they were supposed to be absorbing the wonderful things around them.

Denise almost said, Sorry, but she didn't, because even though she did not know what to say, she knew she did not want to say that.

And Cliff kept staring at her. He seemed to be wondering if his little outburst had spoiled his chances. And Denise supposed that he did think he'd ruined it for himself, because he said to her, evenly, smoothly, in a voice slightly lower than regular talking, "I spent a fortune on this goddamn outfit. And the ticket. And the parking. I thought you were into this. You're a little freak. You know that? You're crazy. You're a loony. I thought this would be fun. For us to fool around here. But you're nuts."

She tried to move her head away, to look out at the ride passing her by. But she couldn't stop gazing on him. She was numb.

"You're delusional," he said. "De-lu-sion-al," he echoed.

But she didn't budge. Didn't break down. Didn't move her gaze. Didn't show anger or shock or sadness. Just stared at him. Stared at this spectacle belittling her, this graying man in the ride's gray light, this graying man cloaked in the princely tassels she'd wanted him to wear. And she didn't give him the joy of showing her sadness, but she was saying to herself, You are so stupid, You are so so stupid.

Then the ride was over. Then the safety bar lifted up away from the passenger car, and Denise bolted away from him, not quite running but doing what she could in her gown and heels, appearing like a blue bell blurring out of the ride, zipping down the path leading to New Orleans Square and then to Adventureland and then to Main Street, U.S.A. and then to the exit and the tram and the parking structure and her car.

In her car, once she had pulled out of the parking structure and emerged onto regular roads, she allowed herself a cry. She drove the familiar route from Disneyland to her house, the route she did so often on days when she needed a release after work, when she needed an escape from figures and her weekday routine, when she would think to herself while at her desk, What the hay, I think I'll go to Disneyland tonight and walk around a bit.

She pulled her car into her garage and entered her house. Bruno was standing in his kennel wagging his tail. She normally let him out immediately after walking in. And Bruno would always squirm with excitement, having heard the garage door sliding upward, then downward, anticipating his release and the kisses she always bombarded him with. But now she walked past his kennel and stopped in front of the hallway mirror.

Now she stared at herself, her tear-ruined makeup, her powder blue gown—ridiculous gown, she thought. Ridiculous girl. Ridiculous woman. And she tore the gown off herself, tearing it to release her body. And the gown crumpled at her ankles, and her round flesh sparkled, gleamed with anger at herself and at him. And she stepped over the gown, and she kicked off her shoes. And in her bra and her underwear and her stockings she bent over and scooped up the dress. Bruno barked, and she ignored him. Bruno barked again, and she turned and yelled, "Quiet!"

Cradling the dress, she marched to the sliding-glass door and stepped outside. It was dark. But in the haze she could make out her familiar things. She made her way to the fire pit and threw the torn gown on top. She started the gas and the spark, and the flames bit into the crumbled mass, and the flames were blue and orange, and the powder blue dress grayed and grayed, and Denise picked up the parts flowing over the edges and tossed them to the center. And like that, the dress was gone. But the fire burned steadily without the dress. Burned steadily with the gas flowing up from the ceramic wood that served as decoration.

Straight-faced, Denise walked back into the house. Straight-faced, she opened her special closet and removed her two other gowns, dragging them by the hangers, letting them scrape across the backyard pavement and swoosh across the damp grass until she reached the flames and, one at a time, hoisted a gown onto the flame and watched the ashes collect among the fake wood and sometimes flit away on a passing breeze. The flames made quick work of the gowns. The fabric was eaten up, inhaled by the fire, and Denise thought to do something while it happened, to be ceremonial about, to dance around the circle and add to the spectacle, but she just stood there in her underwear, sweating and watching, sweating and wondering how it had come to be that this was where she was and what she was doing.

The minutes passed, and eventually her body made clear its tiredness, her legs and feet, and even her shoulders from all that posturing. She turned off the fire pit and went back inside. She remembered Bruno and let him out of his kennel. He was not hesitant. He leapt up on her, and she scooped him up and squeezed him before setting him down. Then she sat on her couch in her bra and underwear and stockings, and she thought to go upstairs to her bedroom but she couldn't. Then she thought to turn on the TV but she couldn't. Eventually she slid from sitting to lying, and she managed to pull a thin blanket over her body when it began to shiver, and she managed to curl into a ball without falling off the couch, and Bruno curled up at her feet as soon as she'd made space for him.

When she slept on her living room couch, she dreamed things that she would remember over coffee in the early hours. She dreamed that she was burning her dresses again, and she was chuckling and lifting her arms up to the gray sky, and she was naked and her hair was in a braid with flowers and she was gliding around the flame, which stretched forty or fifty feet into the air, and her movements were like water and her skin was the texture of an aloe leaf. And there was an endless supply of gowns, and she kept feeding them to the flames, blue gowns, purple gowns, pink gowns, yellow gowns, all encrusted with jewels, all finely stitched, showing intricate patterns at the breast or at the thighs, often with flowers or butterflies, but all of them, all of them, fed to the flames one at a time while she floated in a circle with skin gleaming. While this was happening, the neighbor boy was peering over his side of the fence, staring at her, falling in love with her except that he was already in love with her from when he had seen her frolicking in the daylight from an earlier time. So he was falling more in love with her and differently in love with her. And while she glided around and commanded the flames, sending dress after dress into the pit, she knew he was watching her, and she knew that he loved her, but she did not let him know she was aware of him. And so she let him watch her burn the many gowns while she swayed and glided and chuckled. And then the dream shifted to the next morning just like that, and she walked barefoot into her backyard, which was full of wildflowers instead of grass and had a pond in the center instead of a fire pit, and along the back fence, which was her usual fence, there was an envelope stuck to the wood, and she opened it, and there was a crayon drawing of a phoenix surrounded by flames, and the boy was all of a sudden standing in front of her, and last night he had been a teenager in love with her, and now he was a little boy, and he said, I drew that for you. It's my favorite mythological creature, the phoenix. But I also like dinosaurs and martians and even fairies. And she picked up the boy and cradled him at her chest, and he nuzzled into her neck, and then she put him down and he skipped over the flowers and crawled up the fence and went home.

Denise woke on the couch and smelled her own sweat. She made coffee and sat in her breakfast nook, sipping and thinking about the dream she remembered so vividly, and thinking too about her date, which for some reason was already slipping out of her memory, seeming less real than the boy's drawing, less real than the warmth on her neck when he nuzzled into her to absorb her scent and softness. Denise would shower soon. She would finish this cup of coffee and then let the water and soap work themselves into her skin and hair, and then she would put on her bathrobe and slippers and make herself some eggs over-easy and toast with apricot preserves, and call her sister and maybe get to talk to her niece and nephews, and maybe call her parents, and talk only about good things. But before she would do all those Saturday things, she would finish this first cup of coffee. And now while sipping, she reached for her phone. Now while the mug was still producing steam she dialed the number of her alteration-shop client, leaving a message on the machine since the store was not yet open, leaving a message explaining that there had been a mistake, an accident, actually, with her gowns, and that she would need to start again and place another order, please, if she had time to give her.

# PUP!

The puppies are back at WBC, and I'm third in line. This is one of the many reasons I chose to go here. Chose to go to Western Baptist. Because they care about us and our stress levels. They get how tough it is to be a college student these days. I've got three finals *and!* three papers due in the next *four!* days, but the puppies are here all week from 10 to 6, and I've got *two!* vouchers for the puppy pen, and then of course there's the taco truck and the *funnel cake truck!* both taking meal swipes, and there's the sumo wrestler padded arena thing, and there's the jumbo fantasy castle bounce house. I'm just saying, it looks like a carnival on the grass quad, but in seriousness, final exams are approaching and we're all just a little stressed out here. For me, it was a no-brainer to use my vouchers on the puppy pen. Let the silly boys wrestle their stress away in that sumo gear.

I'm checking my phone and it's *10:13!* and in two minutes—*two minutes!*—it'll be my turn to *de-*stress. They let twelve students in at a time, and there are *twelve puppies!* in there. I got here just after 9:30 and was fifteenth in line, and then at 10 on the dot a puppy worker opened the gate and twelve stressed-out students darted toward those scrumptious pups.

Oh those pups are so scrumptious, and I'm watching them wrestle and play with my fellow stressed-out peers, that lucky dozen, and *oh my!* that one's licking her face, lucky duck, lucky pup girl, and I'm studying the faces of all those cuties and figuring out which one I'm gunning for, and *oh sweet Saint Lucy!* the puppy workers are corralling the stressed-out students, who do in fact look less stressed-out after their puppy time, but too bad we still have those pesky finals ahead, but no matter because now the gate is opening for my group, and I feel the same kind of giddy as when I'm at Disneyland and my group is let in to the Dumbo ride and I rush in to find the perfect Dumbo to climb in, preferably one with a pink bow, but purple and yellow are also desirable colors.

The gate opens, and the three in front of me rush in, and once they're out of my way, I make a beeline for the pup with brown floppsy ears and white spots on her nose, and I would have settled for the pup with golden floppsy ears over there, *but who am I kidding?* this is the pup I've been longing for, and I swoop her up in my arms—*oh him!*—and I nuzzle him under my chin and then bury my face in his tummy, and my nose grazes his little boy parts, *but oh well!* and then I move him into the crook of an arm, and I sit criss-cross while rocking him and then nuzzling him and then rocking him and then nuzzling him. I could live with my face in this pup's belly. This is what I want all the time. All the time I want this little guy's tender skin and pup fur relaxing my face.

But now I'm being nudged by a puppy worker, and there's no way fifteen minutes have passed, but the puppy workers are corralling everyone in my group, and my fellow stressed-out college mates are heading for the gate, having relinquished their pups to the green well-maintained grass, and some of them look somewhat de-stressed, blowing air kisses as they depart from the heavenly pen, but not me. *Not me!* I stand, but I've still got my little guy smushed to my face, so I move him into my chest, and I'm trying to tell this puppy worker that I'd like to use my second voucher now too. But he's saying, *Back of the line, miss,* and I'm reaching for my second voucher, but he's not having it. So I back away while guarding my pup, and two other puppy workers approach me, saying *Miss, miss, please set him down,* miss, but I'm not done yet.

I turn my back to them, and there's the freshmen dorms in the distance, and I'm off, leaping out of the pen like a protective momma, bolting across the grass toward home-away-from-home until I'm brought down like prey, someone's arms ensnaring my calves, my chest and cheek smacking against the manicured lawn amid gasps and a yelp.

# THE WILDNESS OUTSIDE MEDIOCRE VILLAGE

We'd been hiking for six hours when we came to Mediocre Village, which is in Station 5 and therefore about 5,000 feet up. It was about noon when we'd made it there to the halfway point. Like the rest of the tourists, we'd been dropped off at the base of Mt. Horenai at 6 am, when the mountain officially opens for business. We'd stood in a small crowd outside the main gate, eager for the mountain to open since we'd gotten up so early to come here, to come for this time to be alone with each other and recharge—recharge, you know, because we'd been snapping a bit but still loved each other. "Let's go to the mountain this weekend," she'd said. "Brilliant," I'd said.

The base of the mountain, miles and miles of it, I imagine, is encircled in a twenty-foot-tall fence. And at the entrance where we were standing— me and Masha, Masha and I—well, at the entrance there, our tickets in our hands, a siren sounded and then a voice said, "Warning. Warning. Gate is about to open. Step away from the gate." And the massive gate started sliding back, creaking on its metal wheels until there was a ten-foot-wide space to pass through. With the girth of that fence, you'd think you're about to enter a prison but then that thought goes away when you see the majestic mountain in front of you. So we passed through the gate, walked up to the turnstile, let the lady scan our three-day/two-night tickets, and we were off to the mountain.

We'd already purchased our walking sticks, backpacks, bottled water, and energy bars ahead of time, and we'd already changed into our hiking gear in the parking lot before boarding the shuttle, so while other folks stocked up at Supply House No. 1, we were among the few folks off to hike the mountain right after the front fence slid open. Of course some folks were on the mountain already if they purchased overnight passes and slept in mountain huts or one of the two hotels, but we were the first ones heading out from the base that day, eager to rise to 10,000-plus feet over the course of two days. The base where the shuttle drops you off at Station 1 is about 700 feet above sea level, so we were looking at gaining about 4,500 feet on Day One and 5,000 feet on Day Two.

So we got to Mediocre Village around noon and were wiped because we'd barely taken any of the courtesy escalators. According to the pamphlet we received at the turnstile, the courtesy escalators were originally installed for staff use only, making it easier for employees to empty out the many trash and recycle bins up and down the mountain. But because so many of the paying hikers were hopping over the rope barrier to ride the escalators and catch a breath, the mountain's management decided to open up the escalators to everyone. But the signs everywhere still encouraged walking. *Glide a While / Then Hike a Mile*, some signs said. *Stand When Beat / Then Move Your Feet*, said others.

Because we didn't use the escalators much, we did make sure to stop and rest at each station. With each 1,000-foot increase we followed the pamphlet's Steps for Easing into Higher Altitudes, which consisted of *1) Drinking water, 2) Stretching (see Diagram A on inside flap), 3) Doing deep-breathing exercises (see Diagram B on inside flap), and 4) Eating three Chewable Mt. Horenai 1000-Foot-Increase Vitamins (available at all Supply Houses and Vending Machines)*. So at each station, we took fifteen minutes or so to acclimate to the new height and to check out each new gift shop. At Station 2 I bought a new hiking stick with a sharper point, at Station 3 we decided to take a twenty-minute power nap in a quick-stop mountain hut, and at Station 4 Masha caved in and bought the "I Climbed Mt. Horenai" sweatshirt she'd eyed at the last gift shop (they don't start selling "I Climbed Mt. Horenai" shirts, sweatshirts, backpacks, stickers, keychains, or license-plate holders until Station 3, and that seems right to me so when you see someone sporting one of those things you know they really did put in a few hours on the mountain).

So by the time we got to Station 5 and walked into Mediocre Village, we were famished. And here's where the story gets interesting. Here's where things started to shake up and where Masha bolted out on her own. We'd had reservations at the Mediocre Hotel, and we had another good laugh about that. I said predictable stuff like, "I hope the room's not mediocre," and Masha said more clever things like, "I hope the sheets aren't midgrade" and "I hope the tub's not of middling size." So we were about to check in and put our packs in our room and then shower and get a bite to eat at the Mediocre Restaurant (more laughing, of course, when we saw that sign out front, and I said, "I hope the food's not mediocre," and she said, "Or that the portions are halved"), but then before we checked in together, I said, "I'm glad you decided to be reasonable and come." And how I let that slip out, I don't know. And in my head I was saying, Dumbass, dumbass, you dumbass. And I quickly sputtered out, "Isn't this fun. Isn't this beautiful. The trees and whatnot. The boulders over there. Pretty scenic, right?"

But of course there was no recovering. Not right away. And she said, "Reasonable." And that's all she said for a moment, and that's all she needed to say. And then I just said, "Sorry," softly, like sheepishly soft. But she shook her head and said she needed more time and said she's going to go get her own mountain hut at Station 6, eat from the vending machines, head out early and have some time to think. "Please let me have some time," she said. "I love you, but I still need more time for all of this." And she said she'd catch up with me at the summit tomorrow evening, maybe around 6 pm, and then we could talk again. Then with the summit air in our lungs and our heads clear from exercise, then we can talk again over dinner. And I knew better than to try and stop her. I just let her go. Because what could I do? She needed space. She needed time away from me. So she bolted to Station 6, and I checked in at the Mediocre Hotel because I was beat and wanted to see what the room looked like anyway.

The room was a room just like any hotel room, the only difference being it was halfway up a mountain. I showered, put my dirty clothes in the mini-washer, took out my second set of clothes from my backpack. Then I took a nap in our bed—well, my bed, I guess—took a nap, then went down for dinner, and even though I was sad about Masha needing some time away from me, it was a good thing that I've never been the type to be insecure about sitting alone in a restaurant.

I walked right up to the hostess and said, "Just one tonight. Just me." And she gave me a nice two-top by the koi pond. The bubbles were pretty soothing. And then when the waiter came over, I said, "Okay, my good man, I'm not going to crack this menu. Just talk to me. Just tell me what's what. I'm a steak man, but I can be swayed."

And he said, "Our steaks are thin on account of most of our guests being fitness buffs. The only cut is one inch, but the meat is divine. We're talking one-hundred-percent grass-fed beef, and we only get flanks. That's what I'd recommend. It's thin but a good portion, and you get roasted vegetables on the side, and you can round out the meal with a starter salad if you'd like. Perhaps the house greens with a raspberry vinaigrette?"

And I said, "Yes, now you're talking. All of that."

And he said, "To drink?"

And along with the standard ice water I ordered a light lager that had a hint of lemon. It was nice. Refreshing. Went well with the steak and veggies. I think he called it a Wezzenheisen or maybe a Weisenhezzen. Anyway, German sounding maybe. Something European. Really good beer. And I ate and drank and did little calf stretches under the table. At one point a good-looking couple sat at the table by me, so I chatted with them a little bit, making small talk, but they had a quick meal and didn't stick around for too long. So I finished my meal looking at the fish and looking around the room and wondering what Masha was up to in her mountain hut.

When I returned to my room, I put my clothes in the mini-dryer, and when they were done I thought about checking out early and doing some night hiking since that was a new feature, a big advertising campaign to draw more folks to Horenai. "Come explore the newly renovated hiking trails at Mt. Horenai," one commercial said. "With two times more handrails than before, and now with night-time hiking available thanks to our newly installed high-end path lights." So I thought about checking out those path lights even though I'd seen pictures, and I thought about hiking to get ahead of Masha so I could go slowly the next day and hopefully have it so she'd have to run into me along the way and perhaps cause an early makeup. But I was still beat on account of not being in hiking shape, so I just went to bed and set my alarm for an early wakeup.

The fight was an aftershock from the previous week, when we'd gotten into it about something small—washing dishes, doing laundry—something like her saying, "Do you think you could just wash that dish quickly?" when I put a dirty dish in the sink, dripped some water on it, and then left it. And I grumbled something about working full time when she works part time, and we let that drop but then she snapped at me about something else, and then it all came out, all the underlying resentment that makes the little fights easier to pick. Well, she was upset that I'd been hanging out with her younger sister Sophie after she—my wife, Masha—had gone to bed. And I said, "Wait. Wait. No way you're mad at me for that. Was it not you who A) told Sophie she should live in our backhouse until she got on her feet, B) told Sophie she should feel free to come into the house whenever she wanted to eat food and/or watch TV, and C) lastly, was it not you who said to me, 'Dear, I want you to be sweet to her and show her how a true gentleman acts after what that prick did to her'?"

She responded by talking about her little sister not knowing boundaries and wearing skimpy shorts on the couch while sitting crisscross, and she said, "You know I can't stay up as late as you. I try but fall asleep. But I don't need to see my husband on the couch with my sister in practically her underwear before I go to bed." And she said, "Maybe you married the wrong sister. Maybe you'd rather be with her."

And in private, not in front of Sophie, in private, back in our bedroom, I said to Masha, "I certainly did not marry the wrong sister. Your sister is crazy." But I shouldn't have said that because, on the one hand, family sticks up for each other, rightfully so, so she got mad at me and defended her sister moments after she'd been knocking her. But the other reason I shouldn't have said that thing about her sister being crazy, the on-the-other-hand part of it was, well, I should have said something nice about Masha and being married to her instead of saying why I wouldn't want to be with Sophie. And I recognized that a little late, and I tried to say some nice things, but the shit had hit the fan, so to speak, and well, there was no cleaning things up that night. But things mellowed out over the next day or two, and that was when Masha had said, "Let's go to the mountain this weekend." So we let her sister stay in the house for the weekend instead of just the backhouse. And we both took vacation time for Monday and Tuesday. Well, I took vacation time because I have a real job. I mean a full-time job. And Masha got her shifts covered for Monday and Tuesday. Our plan was to leave early Saturday morning, which we did, and then to sleep at the Mediocre Hotel Saturday night and the Summit Hotel Sunday night, and then walk down the whole mountain on Monday and make it back to our place Monday night. We'd kept Tuesday open for a rest-the-legs day. So we'd booked the two nights at the two hotels and purchased three-day mountain passes online, and we were chipper

Saturday morning, setting out to do this thing together, spending time together in nature and everything, and we were having a good Saturday together before I said something stupid and Masha stormed off right after we'd reached Mediocre Village.

So I spent Saturday night in the Mediocre Hotel by myself, and then I got up at a decent hour, but not as early as I'd hoped, and I suspected that I wouldn't be able to catch Masha since she'd be starting a station ahead of me, so I just packed up my bag, tightened my laces, and spent the day walking to the summit to meet up with her around 6 pm as planned. There's no reason to go on and on at this point in the story. I walked and walked and walked. Was it beautiful? You bet. The treeline of Mt. Horenai is pretty high, actually, since the area gets decent rain. The trees stop somewhere after Station 8, so maybe around 8,500 feet or so, and before I got to that point, it was the regular beauty—trees, boulders, shrubs—and it was fairly private, but sometimes I'd pass a cluster of people or get passed by some folks. But mostly on Day 2, and that would have been Sunday, I just walked with my head down and powered on, seeing mostly the dirt trail, and I was better about avoiding the courtesy escalators whenever the path curved and I saw one. I just walked, gave Masha her time, wondered if she missed me, wondered if she felt bad or good after bolting.

After the treeline ended it was crazy because the Summit Hotel really stood tall like a beacon up there once you're not seeing it through trees but just by itself. And I was grateful Masha and I purchased thin but wind-resistant—and surprisingly warm—jackets because it was way windier up top. I got to the summit in the early afternoon. I was exhausted. I'd made just two stops. At Station 8 I'd refilled my two bottles at one of those card-swipe water machines. And at Station 9 I popped into the last supply house before reaching the shops at Summit Village. I was looking for something to give Masha, something that said, Sorry I'm not very thoughtful sometimes but am also most of the time still desirable and easy to be around. Maybe like a panda with hiking boots on. All I could find was a hat that had *Wildness Is a Necessity* printed inside the outline of a mountain. I bought it, thinking it might do but also suspecting there would be more things up ahead at the summit.

So as I said, I got to the summit and it was still light and pretty warm except for the cool breeze, and there were people scattered all around, taking pictures from being so high up—10,326 feet, to be exact—the tallest peak within a four-hour drive and pretty reasonably priced compared to some of the other mountains. But I didn't see Masha anywhere, so I sat on an empty bench, and let me tell you, then I felt sore, like all at once. And I just sat there in the open, looking around at the people dotting the terrain, waiting to recognize or to be recognized.

A few hours passed, and no Masha. I tried her cell phone, but there was no response. It went straight to voicemail. I sent a text but wasn't expecting a reply, at least not right away. And here's the gist of the night. After sitting on that bench for a long time, I got up—was so sore—and walked around the summit in a circle—surprisingly long walk around, what with all the little photo-ops and shops and the hotel in the middle. So I walked around the summit four times, and that took a long time, and I had my eyes peeled for Masha, but nothing. So finally I went inside the hotel, spoke to the front-desk clerk to see if maybe Masha checked in without me, but she hadn't checked in yet, so I checked myself in and made sure to tell the guy that my wife—that Masha—would be checking in too, so please just give me one key, I said, and keep the other here for her.

One funny thing was that the Mediocre Hotel was nicer on the inside than the Summit Hotel, and I wished Masha had been there to joke about that with me. And the Mediocre was probably nicer and bigger because more people stayed there and not as many people would make it all the way to the Summit. Like probably people start hiking, intend to carry through to the top, but then after staying a night at the halfway point just decide that that was good enough and then head back down the mountain. But so anyway, the Summit Hotel looks spectacular from the outside, all lodge-like and rustic looking since it's in all the advertisements, but really the inside is outdated and tacky. Old lamps with fraying tassels. Too much brown everywhere. Too much brown and tan. The carpets, the drapes, the comforter.

So Masha never showed that night. I was worried. I was beyond worried. I knew her impromptu plan for Night One: sleep in her own mountain hut, then meet up with me the next night. Well, that day came and went and I spent the second evening going in and out of the hotel, walking around the summit, then checking back at the front desk and the room, and then going out again. No Masha. Finally I ate at the hotel restaurant, but I couldn't enjoy myself, not like the first night when I could kind of relax knowing there was a plan. So I ate a dinner—the Summit's famed grilled salmon—and it was good, had a basic lemon and garlic sauce, but I didn't really chat with the waitress or any of the other diners, wasn't really enjoying myself. Just sat there, ate, then got back to wandering.

I convinced myself that Masha must have been too tired to make the summit that day, so she just stopped at a mountain hut at Station 8 or 9, maybe even back at 7, to rest and then probably just decided to stay one more night alone and make the summit the next day. And I thought I wouldn't be able to sleep that second night since I was worried about her, but I was exhausted, my body, but also my head after worrying, so when I got in that bed—and I must admit that the bed and sheets were super comfortable even though the comforter was tacky, brown with tan swirls—but so when I got in that bed, I conked out, just like that, no half-asleep middle time, no trying to fall asleep, just bam, in bed, then asleep. And then morning. And I'd forgotten to set my alarm, and I was sleeping sleeping sleeping, and a glow woke me up, and I thought it was the sun. But the curtains were closed, and the glow that woke me came from Masha's face.

She was standing over me, just staring at me, and her face glowed. It was glowing. It was radiant like the sun, as corny as that sounds. That's the best way to describe it. Radiant like the sun. Her face was radiant, and I was shocked and disoriented and wondered if I was dreaming or if there was something wrong with her.

"Hey," she said. "Sorry I didn't answer your calls or texts. I didn't get them until today. I turned my phone off and kept it in my pack."

I sat up in bed, slid a pillow behind my back and leaned against the headboard. "Are you okay?" I asked. "You're glowing. Your face, your skin, it's like a lightbulb. Did you know that?"

"I saw in the mirror." She nodded toward the bathroom. "I've been here for a half-hour or so, took a shower, wanted to watch you sleep for a while but I guess my face woke you up."

"Does it hurt?"

"It feels good," she said. "I feel good. The girl who handed me my room key. She asked that too. She leaned over the counter and gave me my key, then softly asked, 'Does it hurt?' And she said, 'I've heard of that happening, but I never believed it.' And I told her I didn't know what she was talking about, and she told me to go look in the mirror. And you'd think I would freak out or something, but you know, when I saw the shine all over my face, I wasn't surprised. I guess part of me knew it was happening even though I couldn't see it. Like how I was feeling was probably reflecting outward too."

We sat there on the bed, me with my legs still under the covers, her leaning toward me with a palm pressed on the comforter. And it would have been dark in the room except that her face provided light. Even though the sun had risen and it was late morning, it would have been dark in the room due to the thick curtains. But it was like her face was its own lamp.

I said, "What do you think caused it?"

She didn't know. Said she didn't do anything.

"What did you do?" I said. "And I'm sorry, by the way. I'm sorry for the other day. And for other things."

"You're fine," she said. "I love you. You know that. But I needed to be away from you. And now I'm happy to be here with you."

"Ok," I said.

"I didn't stay in a mountain hut," she said. "Two days ago, when I left you at the hotel, I kept walking, but I didn't stay in a mountain hut."

"Where'd you stay?"

"I made it to the summit on the first day. After I left you, I was going to stop at Station 6. Actually I was going to turn back at first, but then I got into a rhythm and just thought that maybe we needed some time. So I was surprised how quickly I made it to 6, and then I just kept going and eventually made it to 7, and I kept drinking a lot of water and getting refills, and I don't know what it was, but for some reason I just kept going, and I made it to the summit while the sun was setting. And then I finally sat. I'd been walking the whole time, or standing to refill the water bottles, but I finally sat up at the summit during sunset. And the sky was orange and purple—"

"Is that when your face starting glowing? From the sunset or something?"

"No. I think it happened yesterday or maybe this morning."

"You should have slept here Saturday night," I said. "Or, I mean, that was an option."

"I thought about it. I was sitting on one of the benches looking out at the sky and down at the trees below, and I was loving the breeze because my body was still so warm from a full day of walking. And I did have that thought. I thought I could see if I could check in up here a day early and we could pay for an extra night. But do you remember that spot between Stations 8 and 9 where the terrain gets real steep with all the rocks?"

"Yeah."

"Well," she said, "I remembered seeing this rock formation off around the side, where the escalator stops and then doesn't start again for a while. And it looked cave-like. And I don't know why, but I just thought of stories, you know, stories from past times, when people would sometimes just hunker down in a cave for no reason. Or, I mean, for reasons. They had reasons. But, you know, they would just go off and hunker down in a cave for this reason or for that. And that's all it took."

"All it took for what?"

"To go back and sleep in that rock area."

I asked, "Are you hurt?" and then thought to look over her body, kind of eyeing her for injuries or bruises I guess. All I'd been able to focus on was the light coming off her face. But she looked fine, unhurt.

And she said, "No. I'm fine. They were just boulders. I walked back down to where they were. And it was dark then and so the path lights turned on—"

"Are those nice? Was it magical walking at night like that on the mountain? I thought about doing that."

"Yeah, I mean, the lights were helpful. I could see where I was walking, so that was good. But so I made it down to that rocky area where the path gets much slimmer, and then I looked around to see if anyone was watching, and I went off course and started climbing sideways on the boulders. I mean not actual climbing, but hovering low to the ground and using my hands too to crawl slowly out of the marked areas. And I walked like that, wrapping around the mountain, until the path lights were far away and the path was far away and I couldn't hear any of the other hikers or anything at all. I just kept going. And then it was black except for that little piece of the moon that was out, but, I mean, it was black compared to what I'd just come from. And it was silent. That's the thing. There wasn't any humming, like the humming all around us all the time that is sound but doesn't seem like sound. Like now."

She paused and tilted an ear, and I mimicked her, and we both acknowledged the humming with a nod.

"It was just really silent out there."

"And you slept in a cave?"

"It wasn't really a cave. I just kept going until I felt like I'd left the world. It's hard to describe. But I felt like I reached another place somehow. Like I was not even on the same mountain or in the same world exactly. I don't know what I'm saying really. But I found this place. And it wasn't a cave exactly. It was a kind of overhang. A crag? Is that the right word? It was like an overhang, and beneath the rock jutting out there was a flat space, maybe a square of like ten-foot by ten-foot. And I stretched out on my back. I'd set my pack down already. So I stretched out on my back, and even though there was the above crag I could still see the sky outward, and I put my arms behind my head, and I stayed awake like that for a few hours, just staring out, and then I slept there like that."

"And could you sleep? Were you scared?"

"I slept great. But only for a few hours. I just needed a few hours. I could tell. I'd already turned my phone off and put it in the bag. I didn't ever know the time. But I could feel like maybe I'd slept two, three, four hours max. Mostly I was just awake and still. And I wasn't scared at all. And you know how they say all the wildlife has been gone from Horenai for years now. Well, I felt things moving around me. I mean, I heard things like whispers and felt like there was movement. Maybe animals. Maybe something else. I don't know. But I felt a stirring, and I wasn't afraid, and I just stayed like that all night."

"And in the morning? What did you do?"

"Nothing."

"Nothing?"

"I woke, and I stretched, and I saw the light breaking the clouds. And I thought about heading back up to the summit, and then I thought about walking down the mountain to meet you. I did think about you. But the truth is, I didn't want to leave that place. That flat square of rock. I wasn't ready to leave it. And I spent the whole day there. Sitting, standing, stretching, lying down. I had a few sips of water now and then but nothing else. I just spent the whole day without moving off that rock. And then I slept there again, and spent the morning there again, and then I finally left in the early day and crept up on you in this bed."

"And your face?"

"I don't know when it happened. Maybe it was gradual over the last two days. Maybe it happened the moment I stepped off the rock."

"Will it last? People will talk. People will be asking about it."

"I'm not sure. It doesn't hurt. That's all I know. And I was thinking in the shower a minute ago. I was thinking that I'd never even know my face was glowing except for others. I mean, it sounds simple, but it seemed profound when I was thinking it. Like I could have gone days and days without ever knowing I had a glowing face until someone else pointed it out to me. Anyway, it's just what I was thinking."

"I'm glad you came back," I said. "I'm glad you decided to come back here."

"I am too," she said.

And then we didn't talk much, and I got out of bed, and Masha slid open the curtains, and a different light filled the room, but her face was still the brightest thing. Like when she walked around, her brightness pushed aside the other light that was there.

We got our packs ready and checked out. It was Monday around noon when I checked out of the room and the two of us walked out of the Summit Hotel together. People stared at Masha. People stared but didn't approach us. People took pictures from a distance, whispered things to each other. We walked down the mountain in one day as we'd originally planned. We stopped for water but nothing else. We made it to the base when the sun was beginning to set. We boarded the shuttle and sat side-by-side while onlookers looked on but didn't ask. No one took pictures in the shuttle. I wondered how the pictures would turn out that were taken during the day. Would people's phones show an orange glow on Masha's face, or would it not show up? Would she look like those ancient paintings where some folks had bursts of light above their head or shooting all around them or even sometimes emanating from their face like Masha?

After we exited the shuttle, we found our car in the parking structure. It was dark in there even though there was still half-light outside. I kept near Masha as we walked to our car, the brightness of her face shining to the left of me. From a distance I imagine it looked like I was standing beside a low streetlight. From a distance I imagine I was the one being shined on and made clear, but up close all I could feel was this aura beside me. When I was near her, I couldn't see much else. When I was near her, my sight was guided by her, directed by her. She drove us home. And we talked a bit on the drive, made small talk, but we also were silent more than usual. I was silent more than usual. Her presence was larger, and I was more controlled in a way, more thoughtful in what I was about to say.

And when we were driving, I wondered what we looked like to other cars on the road. I wondered what drivers thought coming up behind us, thinking from a distance that the roof light was on, thinking from a distance that the interior light was on until they saw rays bursting out of the windows, rays filling the whole car, light screaming from the driver's side in some unimaginable way. And sitting there I thought about the coming days, our lives, our routines, and if things would change and how they might change and how long this would last. I thought about those things, but I also wondered about myself. And I was forming a plan then. I was forming my own plan to sneak away to Horenai for a spell, to leave a note one day and set out at night, scale the fence when the mountain was closed, climb by the sliver of moonlight and find Masha's rock, or another, find some place to wait and wait and wait, and then see if I might stumble across a bit of the old wildness she'd uncovered.

DEREK UPDEGRAFF

# Acknowledgments

My thanks to the editors of the following journals, where these stories first appeared:

"Release from the Ceramic Doghouse" in *The Carolina Quarterly*

"Husky" in *the minnesota review*

"In Olden Times" in *Storm Cellar*

"Dorothy" in *Fourteen Hills*

"Dummy" in *The Greensboro Review*

"The Incident at Our Lady" in *Tikkun*

"It Takes a Village" in *Yemassee*

"Gone" in *Jabberwock Review*

"After So Many Millennia of Birds" in *Big Muddy*

"Audition" in *TSR: The Southampton Review*

"Estate Sale" in *Gold Man Review*

"The Bull from Kelp Forest" in *Raleigh Review*

"At the Dog Park" in *CutBank*

"Cinder" in *North Dakota Quarterly*

"Pup!" in *Hobart*

"The Wildness Outside Mediocre Village" in *Tahoma Literary Review*

I'd also like to thank Kim Verhines at SFA Press for supporting my work yet again.

Thanks as well to my mom and my sister, and all the Updegraffs, Swackhamers, Apgars, and Bells. This book is dedicated to my dad, who had the chance to read most of these stories as they came out in journals; his love of language and literature set off a spark in me long ago that I'm forever grateful for. And most of all, thanks again to Elizabeth and our three daughters, who make life lovely and brimming.

# About the Author

Derek Updegraff has published short stories, flash fictions, poems, and translations in dozens of literary journals. He has been a finalist in the flash fiction contests at *American Short Fiction* and *Bat City Review* and runner-up in *CutBank*'s Big Sky, Small Prose Flash Contest. *Pup! et cetera* is his second book of stories. His debut fiction collection, *The Butcher's Tale and Other Stories* (2016), and his most recent poetry collection, *Paintings That Look Like Things* (2018), are also available from Stephen F. Austin State University Press. He grew up in San Diego and earned an M.F.A. in creative writing from Cal State Long Beach and a Ph.D. in English from the University of Missouri. Also an author of scholarly essays, he is a contributing writer for *The Encyclopedia of Medieval Literature in Britain* (Wiley-Blackwell, 2017). He currently lives in Riverside, California, and is an Associate Professor of English at Azusa Pacific University.